D0045514

by Perdita Finn

Little, Brown and Company
New York ✶ Boston

This book is a work of fiction. Names, characters, places, and incidents are the product of the author's imagination or are used fictitiously. Any resemblance to actual events, locales, or persons, living or dead, is coincidental.

HASBRO and its logo, MY LITTLE PONY, EQUESTRIA GIRLS, and all related characters are trademarks of Hasbro and are used with permission.

© 2016 Hasbro. All Rights Reserved.

In accordance with the U.S. Copyright Act of 1976, the scanning, uploading, and electronic sharing of any part of this book without the permission of the publisher is unlawful piracy and theft of the author's intellectual property. If you would like to use material from the book (other than for review purposes), prior written permission must be obtained by contacting the publisher at permissions@hbgusa.com. Thank you for your support of the author's rights.

Little, Brown and Company

Hachette Book Group

1290 Avenue of the Americas, New York, NY 10104

Visit us at lb-kids.com

Little, Brown and Company is a division of Hachette Book Group, Inc. The Little, Brown name and logo are trademarks of Hachette Book Group, Inc.

The publisher is not responsible for websites (or their content) that are not owned by the publisher.

First Edition: September 2016

Library of Congress Control Number: 2016939316

ISBN 978-0-316-39537-3

10 9 8 7 6 5 4 3 2 1

RRD-C

Printed in the United States of America

For all of Ms. Nunnery's
music students. Keep on singing
about friendship!

CONTENTS

✶ ✶ ✶

CHAPTER

1

A Midnight Nightmare

★ ★ ★

Twilight Sparkle tossed and turned in her bed. She was mumbling in her sleep. "No, it can't be true. It isn't true."

The sun was pouring into her room, but she was fast asleep. She was having a terrible nightmare. She couldn't wake up from it. She didn't hear her friends outside her door.

"Twilight," whispered the soft voice of Fluttershy. "Are you still asleep?"

"If she is, that won't wake her up!" Rainbow Dash pounded on the door. "Twilight," she called. "The bus for Camp Everfree leaves in ten minutes!"

Twilight's brown-purple eyes fluttered open. "Oh no." She gasped. She hadn't even started packing yet. What a nightmare! She leaped out of bed. She threw open her bedroom door. All her friends were there—with their suitcases. "I can't believe I overslept." Spike, her pet dog, yawned.

Sunset Shimmer was shaking her head in disbelief. "Me neither. That's not like you."

"Don't you have a super-annoying alarm clock that goes *ehhh ehhh ehhh*?" Pinkie Pie wondered, looking around.

Twilight lifted her pillow. Smothered

underneath it was her alarm clock—making an annoying *ehhh ehhh ehhh* sound.

Sunset Shimmer clicked it off. "It's gonna be fine," she reassured her friend. "We'll help you pack."

Rarity was rummaging through Twilight Sparkle's closet. She took a gorgeous, shimmering dress off a hanger. She folded it carefully and put it in Twilight Sparkle's suitcase.

Applejack couldn't believe it. "We're going to be out in the woods. When is she going to need that?"

Rarity tossed her mane of long, dark hair. "If we were going to the moon, I'd insist she pack an evening gown. One never knows, darling!"

Each of the girls was rushing around helping Twilight Sparkle pack. Pinkie Pie found an uneaten cupcake and tucked it into a corner of the suitcase. Fluttershy made sure to throw in a few of Twilight Sparkle's favorite stuffed animals. Rainbow Dash took a signed photo of herself playing soccer and placed it on top of the growing pile. Spike dropped in one of his chew toys.

Applejack rolled her eyes. She picked out some pants, long-sleeve shirts, a bathing suit, and a flashlight. That was what was on the official list. That's what you needed at camp.

Twilight Sparkle felt overwhelmed. She still felt groggy and tired. She'd woken up from one nightmare into another. "Let me just get changed," she told the others, grabbing an outfit.

She caught a glimpse of her reflection in the full-length mirror hanging on her closet door. Something was glittering in her eye. Something dark and cold. Something frightening. What was it?

Twilight Sparkle stared at her reflection. Her eyes were becoming darker. Her pink-streaked violet hair was growing wilder. It was almost as if it were highlighted with flames. She was changing. Dark-purple wings were sprouting from her back. In the mirror, Twilight Sparkle had become Midnight Sparkle.

The Equestria Girls backed away from her in fear.

This was the magical monster Twilight Sparkle had turned into at the end of the Friendship Games. She had opened a portal between the enchanted world of Equestria and Canterlot High—that had nearly destroyed them both.

How could this be happening? "Sunset Shimmer helped me defeat you!" Twilight Sparkle exclaimed in desperation.

But Midnight Sparkle was taking over. She gestured toward the mirror. It revealed the terrible moment when Twilight Sparkle had turned into the evil Midnight Sparkle, towering over her classmates. Holes had ripped open in the sky. Jagged cracks had torn apart the front lawn of Canterlot High. Sunset Shimmer had appeared and blasted Midnight Sparkle with her magic. She had called Twilight Sparkle back. She had saved her from the worst part of herself.

The reflection of Midnight Sparkle in the mirror cackled. "You and your friends can never truly defeat me. Midnight Sparkle's a part of you."

The mirror cracked.

Midnight Sparkle leaned out from the mirror toward a terrified Twilight. "I'll always be there," she hissed. "Waiting in the darkest shadows of your mind. I'll be back, Twilight!"

Midnight Sparkle waved her hands and blasted magic out of the unicorn horn on her head. It struck the floor of the room with a lightning bolt. The room began to dissolve. The portal was open again. Reality was disappearing!

The girls screamed.

Midnight Sparkle was triumphant. "And this time I won't stop until I have *all* the magic!" She reached through the mirror and grabbed Twilight Sparkle's hand. They began to merge with each other. Twilight was disappearing, too.

What a nightmare!

"Twilight! Twilight!" barked Spike.

"No! Stop!" screamed Twilight.

"Twilight, wake up!" Spike yelped.

"Stop!"

Twilight woke up with a start. She'd been asleep. The whole time. She wasn't in her room at home. She wasn't late for the bus to Camp Everfree. She was already on the bus—and her friends were all staring at her.

Pinkie Pie giggled. "We can't stop, silly! We're not there yet."

Twilight Sparkle tried to catch her breath. She was shaking. What a terrible nightmare. It wasn't true, was it? She wasn't going to turn into Midnight Sparkle again. She wouldn't. She couldn't. Could she?

CHAPTER

2

Bus-ride
Daydreams

✦ ✦ ✦

Sunset Shimmer was worried about her friend. "Hey, are you okay?" she whispered.

Twilight forced a smile to her lips. "I'm fine," she said.

But Sunset Shimmer wasn't so sure. Once, she had turned into a she-demon and tried to take over Canterlot High just like Twilight Sparkle. She had nightmares afterward, too. It took a long time for her to settle down after that. She was going to keep an eye on Twilight Sparkle.

Pinkie Pie was bouncing up and down in her seat. Her bubblegum-pink curls were bouncing, too. "We are going to have so much fun," she squealed. "We're gonna roast marshmallows and eat marshmallows and sleep on marshmallow pillows!"

Rainbow Dash shook her head. "Probably not gonna do that."

"Maybe *you're* not." Pinkie Pie giggled. She pulled out a squishy marshmallow pillow from her backpack.

At the front of the bus, Principal Celestia clapped her hands. "Attention, students! We're almost there, but before we arrive, we just wanted to say how proud we are of you for raising enough money to go on this class field trip."

Vice Principal Luna was beaming happily beside her. "When we were your age, we made some of our favorite memories in these woods, and we're sure you will, too."

"Now, who's excited for Camp Everfree?" exclaimed Principal Celestia.

All the students on the bus cheered. Except for Twilight Sparkle.

Her dream was distracting her. She stared out the window as the bus rattled deeper and deeper into the woods. The trees were lush and green.

Led by Principal Celestia, the students on the bus were singing.

"Will you be lost by time or part of history?

It's up to you to make the person that you want to be.

Come to a magical place that's full of mystery,

Where you can be part of the Legend of Everfree!"

Each of the girls was daydreaming about her camping adventure. Fluttershy was hoping she would meet all kinds of woodland animals—squirrels and bunnies and owls. Applejack wanted to hike and explore the woods. She wanted to get off the trail and get lost and find her way back to camp all by herself. Pinkie Pie was thinking about marshmallows and how to toast them perfectly so every side was a golden brown and the insides were soft and gooey. Rarity was ready to decorate—her cabin, the trees, the docks. Just because you were out in the wild didn't mean you had to give up your sense of style. She'd brought plenty of scarves just in case. Rainbow Dash imagined racing through the forest. She'd run to the top of the mountain and back again. Sunset Shimmer thought of all the stories they were going to tell and the songs they were going to sing around the campfire. What a wonderful trip it was going to be!

But Twilight Sparkle was worried. The glare of the sun reflected her face back at her through the window. She wasn't turning into Midnight Sparkle, right? She shivered. She couldn't stop thinking about her nightmare.

The other kids were singing again. *"You're more than what you think you are. A shining flame or a dark star."*

Twilight Sparkle gulped. She never wanted to be a dark star again.

The bus was driving deep into the woods. The trees were closer together. They were gnarled and creepy looking. Vines waved like tentacles. The students were excited and a little bit scared. They sang to keep their spirits up.

"The storytellers change, but legends last eternally.

So long as people tell tales of the extraordinary.

And if you play your part, you'll be more than a story,

You will become the Legend of Everfree!"

No one saw the glowing pair of eyes peering through the dark-green leaves. But the eyes saw them. They were ready.

"Hooray!" shouted the campers. An enormous sign announced that they had reached their destination at last. They were at Camp Everfree!

CHAPTER

3

Sunny with Scattered Clouds

★ ★ ★

The Canterlot High students poured off the bus. They unloaded all their bags and suitcases under the direction of Principal Celestia. The sun glimmered on the lake. Birds were singing. The woods didn't feel scary anymore at all.

Fluttershy felt like she was in heaven.

"Isn't Camp Everfree just beautiful?" she enthused. "I can't wait until we have our first nature walk."

Spike wagged his tail. "I definitely wanna go on one of those."

"You want to see all the adorable woodland creatures, too?" she asked him sweetly.

"Yes!" yipped Spike. "Specifically squirrels. More specifically, so I can chase them."

Applejack exhaled happily. "I'm just lookin' forward to roughin' it. I'm gonna make my own shelter, forage for food…"

"You know they provide us with meals and tents, right?" Rainbow Dash laughed.

"Yep," Applejack answered. "Still gonna forage, though."

Rarity was looking forward to sunbathing. "I'm just after some R and R." She sighed. "The past year has all been a little too much for my tastes."

"I'll say," Pinkie Pie agreed. "We fought three evil sirens who tried to hypnotize everybody with their singing, one ridiculously competitive rival school, and two demon fiends!"

Oops! Pinkie Pie slapped her hand over her mouth. She hadn't meant to say that about Sunset Shimmer and Twilight Sparkle. "No offense," she added.

"None taken," said Sunset Shimmer.

But Twilight Sparkle looked upset.

"You'll get used to it," Sunset Shimmer whispered to her.

Applejack stepped in. "Canterlot High has become a regular magic magnet. Gonna be nice gettin' to a place where we don't have to worry about that kind of stuff."

"You said it!" Spike barked. "We definitely aren't going to have to worry about anything strange happening here."

The Equestria Girls all looked at the dog. The *talking* dog.

Spike shrugged. "I mean besides the whole *I can talk even though I'm a dog* thing."

The handsome Flash Sentry headed over to the cluster of girls, a backpack on each shoulder.

"Here you go, Twilight," he said shyly.

Twilight smiled. "Thanks. It's Flash, right?"

Flash's face fell. "Yup," he said, trying to hide his disappointment. "That's me. And you're you. And we don't know each other very well." He stepped back, embarrassed. "Good story," he muttered to himself.

Twilight was confused. Why was he so

upset? What had she done? "Right. I guess I'll see you around."

Sunset Shimmer pulled her aside. "You know how there's that girl who looks just like you when she's here but lives in another dimension where she's a pony princess?"

Twilight nodded, listening.

"Flash kind of had a thing for her," Sunset Shimmer explained.

"Oh!" Twilight's eyes widened.

The PA system was crackling. "Hey, everyone," called out a soft, relaxed voice. "If you could start heading to the courtyard, that would be rad. It's time to start the best week of camp ever!"

Tents and the mess hall surrounded the main courtyard. There were picnic tables on the lawn, a gazebo, a sundial, and a totem pole. A bell rang and the campers headed over to the gazebo, where a young woman was standing on a platform.

Gloriosa Daisy looked cheerful and down-to-earth. With a clipboard in her hands, she also looked very organized. "Hi, everyone!" she said. It was her voice that had come over the PA. "Welcome to Camp Everfree. I'm Gloriosa Daisy, your camp director. Think of me as your friendly camp and nature guide! And this is my brother, Timber Spruce!"

A cute goofball of a teenage boy stepped up to join Gloriosa. He waved at the campers. "Think of me as that awesome guy who should always be invited to fun things."

Gloriosa smiled. "We aim to please, so before we hand out your tent assignments, we'd like to hear from all of you. You're free to do whatever you like here—"

"Except hike near the rock quarry," interrupted Timber Spruce. "That's off limits."

"Yes," agreed Gloriosa, her smile a little less genuine. "But otherwise your options are wide open. So what activities will make this the very best week of your lives?"

Rainbow Dash's hand shot up. "Rock climbing," she announced.

"Done!" exclaimed Gloriosa.

Rainbow Dash's hand shot up again. She didn't wait to be called on. "Archery!"

Gloriosa nodded, her smile still on her face. "Of course."

"Tetherball!" added Rainbow Dash.

"Naturally!" said Gloriosa, but the other girls could tell that she was a little bit irritated.

When Rainbow Dash raised her hand

again, Sunset Shimmer gently pulled it down. "I know you're excited," she whispered. "But maybe give somebody else a chance to make a suggestion."

Reluctantly, Rainbow Dash lowered her hand.

Gloriosa called on Bulk Biceps. "Arts and crafts!" he said enthusiastically. "My mom needs some new pot holders."

"I'll supply the looms," Gloriosa promised. She pointed at Pinkie Pie.

Pinkie Pie was jumping up and down. "Cookie decorating!"

Gloriosa laughed. "I do make a mean sugar cookie."

Fluttershy was called on next. "Early-morning nature walks," she suggested quietly.

Gloriosa looked pleased. "With walking sticks for everyone."

"A fashion show where I design the most fabulous camp looks inspired by today's hottest trends and have them modeled by my classmates in a gorgeous outdoor setting," blurted out Rarity.

Uh-oh, thought each of the girls. Was Rarity going to be disappointed?

She wasn't. Gloriosa was beaming. "A camp tradition," she explained, to Rarity's delight.

Timber Spruce scratched his head, confused. "We have literally never done that."

"Best week of camp ever, remember?" hissed his sister under her breath. Her cheerful smile never left her face. She looked out over the campers. "I'll be taking requests the rest of the time you're here, so if there is anything you'd like to do, anything you need, just ask. I've got this!"

Principal Celestia, who was standing at the back of the crowd of her students, raised her hand. "What about the camp gift? That was my favorite Camp Everfree tradition."

"The camp gift!" Gloriosa clapped her hands. "Of course!"

Timber Spruce was even more confused. "Really?"

"Yes, really," whispered Gloriosa through clenched teeth.

"I just thought—"

Gloriosa glared at him, and he stopped midsentence. "Then you were wrong."

Sunset Shimmer had been noticing the brother and sister's whispered exchanges. "Anyone else picking up on a little tension between Gloriosa and her brother?"

The girls shrugged. Not really. They

were too excited for all of the activities that were about to begin.

Gloriosa was finishing up her introduction. "Here at Camp Everfree, our motto has always been 'Leave the world a little better than you found it.' Every year, campers work together to create something useful. A gift for future campers. Working toward this common goal is key to forming the strong bonds that will last well beyond your time here at camp." She glared for a moment at her brother, Timber Spruce. "Which is why it is so important. This gazebo was a gift from last year's group. And the totem pole and the sundial were also made by campers."

"The sundial was our year's gift," Principal Celestia explained to her students.

"Even though *some people* thought it was

a little impractical, since a sundial can't be used at night," added Vice Principal Luna, her lips pursed.

"That may be true," Principal Celestia said curtly. "But if *some people* had a better attitude about it, they wouldn't have been sent to the Moonstone tent."

"Luckily, *some people* were eventually forgiven for their rash behavior."

The girls listened, wide-eyed, as their teachers sparred. It was easy to forget that they had once been campers just like them.

Gloriosa Daisy cleared her throat to get everyone's attention. "You all seem like a really amazing group, so I'm certain you'll come up with something inspiring to leave behind."

The campers cheered.

"Yeah, we will!" hollered Rainbow Dash.

"Darn tootin'!" Applejack shouted.

"We certainly will," agreed Fluttershy.

"Speaking of leaving things behind," added Timber Spruce, "now's the time when we give out tent assignments, so you can leave your heavy bags...behind."

Gloriosa glared at him.

"What?" Timber Spruce protested. "That's one of my better segues."

"Girls will be getting their assignments from Timber," Gloriosa continued. "Guys, you're with me."

Everyone shuffled over to get his or her cards. Each card had a matching gem on it. Each gem color was a special tent.

"Yay!" Pinkie Pie exclaimed. "I'm in the Emerald tent!"

"Me too!" Rarity smiled.

"Same here!" Rainbow Dash fist-bumped Pinkie Pie and Rarity.

Fluttershy looked a little disappointed when she held up her Amethyst card. None of the other girls were in her tent. She gulped. But at least DJ Pon-3 would be with her. She was always friendly—and she was sure to play great music. DJ Pon-3 gave her the thumbs-up and Fluttershy smiled.

Sunset Shimmer was in the Sapphire tent. Twilight held up a blue card.

"Me too!" she exclaimed, delighted. "I mean, I'm assuming I am. Technically, sapphires aren't just blue. They can be pink, purple, yellow—"

"But they're mostly blue," interrupted Timber, who overheard her. "That's why they're named after the Latin word *saphirus*. That means blue."

Twilight Sparkle looked at him in amazement. It wasn't often that she met someone who was as smart as she was. "I know," she said playfully. "But did you know that sapphires are just rubies without chromium?"

Timber Spruce smiled, impressed. "No, but did you know that Sapphire tent is the best one?"

"No," Twilight Sparkle answered. "Why is that?"

"Because you're in it."

Twilight Sparkle blushed. "I bet you say that to all the campers."

Timber Spruce shook his head, laughing. "Not true."

Bulk Biceps was holding up a red card, looking confused. Timber Spruce went over to him. "You're in the Ruby tent? That's the worst one!" He winked at Twilight.

"*Aww* man!" Bulk Biceps sighed.

"I'm just joking, buddy," said Timber Spruce. "Ruby tent is great. It's like the Sapphire tent with chromium."

Twilight Sparkle laughed. Timber Spruce was so clever.

Timber Spruce draped an arm over Bulk Biceps's muscled shoulder. "The Ruby and Coral tents do look an awful lot alike to the undiscerning eye. I'd better show you where it is."

He glanced back at Twilight. "See you around."

Twilight watched him as he headed toward the tents. A second later, she realized that all her friends were grinning at her.

"What?"

Applejack giggled. "Nothing."

"That was ah-dorable," gushed Rarity.

Gloriosa was hurrying everyone to his or her tent to unpack. "Go get settled in! We'll be meeting at the docks in fifteen minutes to go over some camp safety rules. Let me know if you need anything!"

"I need something." A hulking business-man with bad hair stepped out from behind the gazebo.

Gloriosa rushed over to him, smiling. "Filthy Rich! So nice to see you!" She hast-ily pulled him away from the campers.

"What are you doing here?" she hissed when they were out of earshot. "Camp is just getting started."

Filthy Rich grinned, pleased with him-self. "Just taking in the scenery, Gloriosa Daisy. It's so relaxing."

"Well," spat out Gloriosa, "you can look

around when camp is over. Now, if you don't mind…" She practically pushed him into his waiting limousine.

Filthy Rich got in angrily. "Fine," he sneered.

Gloriosa realized that some of the campers were watching her. She plastered a smile back into her voice. "Filthy Rich is an alumnus of the camp. He likes to check on his old stomping grounds every now and then," she explained. "But enough about him! Find your tents and put away your things! We've got the best week of camp ever to begin!"

She clapped her hands, and the last campers headed to their tents. Only after everyone was gone did she stop smiling.

Gloriosa Daisy was not happy. She was not happy at all.

CHAPTER

4

Magic Gets Off the Ground

★ ★ ★

The sun sparkled on the lake and a light breeze blew through the trees. Each of the tents looked like a jewel on the edge of the forest. Campers were heading into their assigned tents and getting unpacked.

Rarity was sorting through the many different outfits she'd brought. "I'm all for learning safety rules, but I do hope I can get started on my designs for the camp fashion show sooner rather than later."

Applejack looked longingly toward the docks and canoes. "I still can't believe you talked Gloriosa into having a fashion show. We're in the middle of the woods for cryin' out loud. We're supposed to be roughin' it."

Rarity chose to disregard what Applejack had just said to her. "It's clear from Gloriosa's own wardrobe that she appreciates a well-put-together look. Even if we are in the middle of the woods."

"Fair enough." Applejack sighed. "Just as long as you don't put me in one of your fancy-pants outfits."

Rarity bit her lip, trying not to smile.

Applejack looked defeated. "You're gonna, aren't you?"

"Don't worry, darling," Rarity reassured her. "It will absolutely speak to your personal sense of style." Her eyes narrowed as she studied Applejack's outfit. "Only much, much more fashion forward."

"If you say so," Applejack agreed reluctantly.

Over in the Sapphire tent, Sunset Shimmer had unpacked and was trying to figure out why she was feeling so uneasy. "That was weird back there, right? With that Filthy Rich guy?" she asked Twilight Sparkle.

"Hmm?" Twilight Sparkle was distracted. She wasn't really listening; she was thinking about Timber Spruce. "I guess so."

"You care which bed you get?" Sunset Shimmer asked her.

Twilight shook her head, and Sunset Shimmer tossed her sleeping bag onto a

⋆ **41** *⋆*

cot. Twilight Sparkle unrolled her sleeping bag on the cot right next to it. Spike whirled around in circles on the cot, trying to get comfortable.

"One, two, three," Spike counted as he twirled. He might be able to talk, but he was still a dog. He plopped down, his head on his paws, and looked at the girls. "I have no idea why I do that, either."

Sunset Shimmer smiled at him, but she couldn't stop thinking about their arrival at camp. Something was off, but what was it? "I just have this feeling that Gloriosa is hiding something," she said to Twilight. She noticed the faraway look in Twilight's eyes. "Her brother is pretty cute, though."

Twilight blushed. "He's okay."

"Now look who's trying to hide something!" Sunset Shimmer laughed.

"I'm not!" protested Twilight.

Sunset Shimmer smiled at her friend. "I'm just messing with you." But something else was worrying Sunset Shimmer. "You okay? You seemed a little freaked-out on the bus earlier."

"Probably had another one of her nightmares," Spike yipped.

Twilight glared at Spike. "I'm fine."

Sunset Shimmer was tucking her backpack under her cot and didn't notice a tube of sunscreen fall out and roll across the floor. She was listening to Twilight. She could tell she was upset but pretending not to be.

"I mean, what do I even have to complain about?" Twilight was saying. "Ever since I transferred here, everyone from Canterlot High has been really nice and accepting." She took a big breath. "Especially considering what happened at the Friendship Games."

"That wasn't your fault," Sunset Shimmer reminded her. "Principal Cinch is the one who encouraged you to try and use all that magic to win the games for Crystal Prep. You weren't ready to have that kind of power."

Twilight Sparkle did not look relieved.

"But it's over now," continued Sunset Shimmer. "And if there is any group that's gonna forgive you for something that happened in the past, trust me, it's this one."

After all, Sunset Shimmer had once turned into an all-powerful she-demon and stolen a magic crown and everything. But everyone makes mistakes, and she had learned from hers. She had learned about friendship.

Rainbow Dash poked her head into the tent. "You guys coming or what?"

"Be right there," answered Sunset Shimmer. "I just want to put on some sunscreen."

But where was it?

"I could have sworn I packed it," Sunset Shimmer muttered.

Twilight spotted it across the floor. "Found it," she said, pointing.

It was as if a beam of invisible magical energy had flowed out of her finger to the tube of sunscreen. It was floating up off the floor and zooming toward Twilight. What was happening? A hairbrush was levitating. A jar of vitamins. One of the cots. Sunset's eyes were wide in amazement. Spike was frozen in wonder. Twilight Sparkle felt scared.

Out of the blue, all the floating objects dropped.

"Did you do that?" Sunset Shimmer asked Twilight.

"I'm so sorry!" she exclaimed. "I didn't mean to."

But Sunset Shimmer was excited. "How is this possible? I mean, if you were a Unicorn in Equestria, sure, but…" Her voice trailed off. This was a whole new aspect to Equestria magic she'd never imagined.

"I can't believe this," Twilight fretted, upset. "It's terrible!" She was so scared of turning back into Midnight Sparkle—and destroying her brand-new friendships, forever.

"It's amazing," disagreed Sunset Shimmer. "This is great! I mean, we've all ponyed up before, gotten the whole ears and wings and tails thing, shot magical rainbow lasers, but nothing like this has ever happened. How did you do it?"

Twilight shook her head. "I don't know. Maybe I didn't. Maybe it's her."

"What?" Sunset Shimmer's brow furrowed. "Her? Who?"

"Nothing," announced Twilight. "Never mind. Can we just not talk about it? And could you please not bring up this whole levitating thing to the others?"

"Why not?"

"You heard Applejack," Twilight reminded her. "This is supposed to be a place where everyone can get away from magic. I don't want them to know I brought some crazy new kind with me."

"If you really don't want me to, I won't say anything," agreed Sunset Shimmer reluctantly.

"I really don't."

Sunset Shimmer thoughtfully watched

her friend head out of the tent to join the others. "This isn't necessarily a bad thing," she said to herself. She looked at her sunscreen. She went over to it and placed her hands a few inches above it. She scrunched up her face, trying to will the magic to come from inside her. Nothing.

Spike was watching. "I think you're just gonna have to pick it up."

Spike was right. Disappointed, Sunset grabbed the sunscreen. But she didn't let go of her questions. No, there were mysterious things going on at Everfree, and she was determined to get to the bottom of them.

CHAPTER

5

Down at the Docks

***

Hurrying to catch up with Twilight Sparkle, Sunset Shimmer bumped right into Gloriosa.

"I can't believe he would just show up like that," the camp director was saying.

"What did you say?" questioned Sunset Shimmer.

Gloriosa looked genuinely confused. "I didn't say anything." She smiled brightly. "Just here to make sure everyone is headed over to the docks. Did you need something?"

"Nope," said Sunset Shimmer. But she was studying Gloriosa and Gloriosa knew it.

"Because if there is anything I can do to make this week the best week ever, you just let me know," Gloriosa enthused with forced sweetness. "I've got this."

"Thanks," answered Sunset Shimmer matter-of-factly. "I'm good."

When Gloriosa was out of earshot, Sunset Shimmer whispered to Spike, "People that chipper make me nervous."

As if on cue, Pinkie Pie bounced over to join them. "This is gonna be *soooooooooo* much fun!" she exclaimed.

Sunset Shimmer smiled helplessly. "I guess not all people." No one could resist Pinkie Pie's cheerful enthusiasm. No one.

They headed down to the lake to join the other girls. Rarity was stretched out on the dock, admiring the view. "It's beautiful, isn't it? It looks like a diamond shining in the sun!"

"Totally!" agreed Pinkie Pie, sitting down beside her. "We're talking about the lake, right?"

Fluttershy was in heaven. "It is lovely out here. The fresh air. The cool breeze. The birds that land on your finger."

The girls watched in amazement as a bluebird fluttered over to sit on the tip of Fluttershy's finger and chirp to her.

"I think that only happens to you," noted Rainbow Dash.

Near the rickety old dock was a boathouse

with canoes lined up along the wall. There were a few docked sailboats on the beach. Gloriosa, along with the Canterlot High teachers, was helping the campers into life jackets.

"Remember what I said," announced Gloriosa. "Proper water safety attire at all times. Lake activities are available every day until sunset, so if you want to canoe, sail, windsurf, or swim, just let me know."

Twilight put on a life jacket and grabbed a paddle. Applejack was already sitting in a canoe in the water, ready to go with her life jacket buckled.

Fluttershy was tearing apart a piece of bread she had in her pocket and feeding it to some ducks who'd paddled over. Fish swam to the surface, opening and closing their mouths hungrily.

"Aren't they the cutest?" A charmed Flut-tershy gushed.

Twilight was headed out to the end of the dock to meet up with Applejack when her foot went through a rotted board. She almost fell right into the water—but a strong pair of arms reached out to grab her. It was Timber Spruce.

"Whoa! I know I'm charming you, but you don't have to fall for me," he joked.

Twilight stammered out a nervous thank-you in response.

On the shore, Flash Sentry watched the whole rescue operation unhappily. "Guess I can't get too jealous, right?" he said to Sunset Shimmer, who was standing nearby. "After all, she isn't *my* Twilight." He looked upset. "Not that the other Twilight was mine. But we were ... you know."

Sunset Shimmer nodded. "Yeah. I get it. But your Twilight is a princess in Equestria. Hate to break it to you, but that's where she's gonna spend most of her time."

"So you're saying I just need to get over her?" asked Flash.

"Kinda," Sunset Shimmer admitted with a nod. "Yeah."

"Ouch." Flash winced as if the news hurt him. "You're not pulling any punches."

"Not really my style. Sorry."

The adults were out on the dock examining the hole in the boards with concern.

"This is a safety hazard," said Vice Principal Luna. "I suggest we close down the dock for the remainder of camp."

Campers groaned. Did that mean no diving? That wouldn't be any fun.

Gloriosa was very quick to notice the

disappointment. "I'm sure it won't have to be for the remainder of camp. Just needs to be patched up a bit. I've got this!"

Applejack had her own ideas. "Or maybe we do." She gathered her friends. "If you ask me, this whole dock needs to go. Buildin' a new one could be our camp gift. Sure, it benefits us, but a nice, new dock would benefit the future campers, too."

Timber Spruce wasn't so sure. "I dunno. It's an awful lot of work. I wouldn't want you guys to miss out on doing other fun camp stuff because you're so busy building a dock for future campers."

Rainbow Dash nodded confidently. "I hear what you're saying, Timber, but we're Canterlot Wondercolts. We've got a reputation to uphold, and there is no way we are gonna leave this place without contributing the most awesome camp gift ever. I'm with Applejack. Building a new dock is definitely it." She turned to the others. "What do you guys think?"

A resounding cheer was the answer.

Gloriosa was pleased, too. "Looks like it's settled, then."

The only one who was still unhappy was Timber Spruce. "Looks like it."

Sunset Shimmer noticed his reaction—and it just didn't make sense. What was up with those two? Why did they always seem to fight about some hidden secret? What was it?

"That's some tension," she muttered to herself.

No one else seemed to notice, however. The other kids were already busy with plans for the new dock. They were clustered together at a picnic table, bouncing ideas off one another. One girl, a talented artist, was busily sketching.

Twilight studied the drawing. "We can reinforce the foundation," she suggested.

Applejack agreed enthusiastically. "Make it nice and sturdy,".

"And we can add a wood-carved sign that says *Camp Everfree.*" Sunset Shimmer could see it in her imagination.

Fluttershy clapped her hands. "And little boxes of food so you can feed the ducks and fishies."

"We'll add lanterns so you can see at night," said Rainbow Dash.

Vice Principal Luna was pleased. "Great ideas," she said to Principal Celestia.

The artist held up a picture of the new dock—with lanterns, fish-food dispensers, and a carved sign. It looked great. Now all they had to do was build it!

"It's stunning," Rarity gushed. "And will make an absolutely perfect runway for my camp fashion show!"

Applejack glared at her. "More important, it'll be a great place for dockin' canoes and feedin' the wildlife."

"You say tomato...I say perfect place to showcase glamorous boho-chic stylings," said Rarity with a toss of her perfectly brushed hair.

"What do you guys think?" Twilight asked their teachers.

"It's going to be a lot of work," admitted Principal Celestia. "But we can do it."

"Yes!!!" exclaimed Pinkie Pie. "Adult supervision!!"

Everyone burst out laughing.

They had their project—and it was going to be a blast.

CHAPTER

6

Campfire After Dark

✶ ✶ ✶

The campers got to work right away. Both Celestia and Luna were keeping a close eye on safety, making sure no one misused any of the tools. Applejack and Rainbow Dash had pulled off the rotten boards and were hammering new ones onto the supports.

This was just the kind of project

Applejack loved best. She looked over at Rainbow Dash. "Nice hammer," she said. "Where'd you get it?"

"Duh," answered Rainbow Dash. "The toolbox."

Applejack grinned and held up her hammer proudly. "That's cool. I made mine!"

Rainbow Dash rolled her eyes.

Fluttershy and Rarity were painting the little boxes that would hold fish and bird food.

With a happy flourish, Rarity put a last dab of paint on hers. *"Voilà! Poisson!"* she said in French, pointing at the decorated fish she had designed. It wasn't exactly designing couture, but it was still fun.

Pinkie Pie was supervising teams of campers carrying long planks over to the docks. She was skipping back and forth, shouting encouragement. "Come on! We can do this!"

Sunset Shimmer was panting, trying to keep up with her. "I wish I had some of your energy, Pinkie."

"I know!" squealed Pinkie delightedly. "Wouldn't that be amazing? If I could just touch you and you'd be all GO, GO, GO like *meeeee!*" She galloped forward.

Sunset Shimmer stopped to catch her breath. "I take that back. One Pinkie Pie's more than enough."

Twilight was sitting at a picnic table, putting together a lantern. Timber was offering her tips on how to keep it lit.

"Making lanterns out of solar-powered garden lights? Pretty crafty, there, Timber," complimented Twilight Sparkle.

"You think that's crafty?" Timber joked.

"You should see my macaroni art. I'm like the Picasso of noodles."

Twilight laughed delightedly. In addition to being smart, Timber was so funny.

"Hey, everyone," announced Celestia. "You've made a lot of progress, but it's going to be getting dark soon. We can pick this up tomorrow between our other camp activities."

Gloriosa Daisy joined her. "Everyone get cleaned up, and we'll gather by the fire pit at eight to share s'mores and scary stories."

"S'mores!" exclaimed Pinkie Pie. Was there anything better than chocolate and marshmallows? This was what she'd been waiting for.

By the time everyone had gathered together again around the fire pit, the stars were twinkling in the sky. The moon was reflected in the glassy surface of the lake. The flames of the fire sent sparks into the darkness.

Pinkie Pie had a stack of s'mores and was toasting another marshmallow while she listened to Rarity finish up a ghost story. Only Rarity's tale of terror wasn't very terrifying.

"And that's when she looked down and realized she was wearing purple socks with a burgundy dress!" concluded Rarity. She looked from camper to camper expectantly. Why wasn't anyone screaming? It was a horrifying story—to her, anyway.

"Purple and burgundy are in the same color family," she explained.

Still, no one said a word. Snips and Snails clapped politely, but they had no idea what she was talking about.

Applejack stifled a giggle. "That was a terrifying story."

"Yeah," teased Rainbow Dash. "I'm terrified she'll try to tell it again."

Vice Principal Luna invited the other campers to tell stories but no one jumped in—until Timber spoke up. "I have one," he said. "But I'm warning you, you might as well hug a friend now. That's how scary it is."

Fluttershy trembled. "Oh dear." She pulled Spike onto her lap and held him tightly.

Timber cleared his throat and waited until all eyes were on him. "It's time," began Timer Spruce, his voice deep and hushed, "to tell you about the Legend of Everfree."

The fire crackled. An owl hooted. The campers listened, goose bumps prickling their arms.

CHAPTER

7

Spooky Stories

★ ★ ★

Timber described the dark forest his great-grandparents had discovered. The trees grew close. Animals scurried through the shadows. The lake was deep and still. He told them how his great-grandparents knew that this was the perfect place for the nature camp they dreamed about. They set about building it: the mess hall, the docks, the fire pit where they were all sitting.

Timber's voice dropped very low, as if he was sharing a dangerous secret. "But once they started building, *strange* things started to happen."

A gust of wind blew through the trees. Fluttershy shivered.

"One pitch-black night, when the wind was howling," Timber continued, "a tree branch crashed through the roof of their cabin! They screamed and ran outside, only to see a giant creature rising from the earth!"

The campers leaned close. They were enthralled.

"Her skin was made of dirt," said Timber. "She had wild hair like the roots of a tree. Her mouth had jagged rock teeth, and her eyes were pools of black tar. But her aura shimmered like diamonds. Anywhere she went, she left a trail of gem dust in her wake." He paused dramatically for a moment.

Some of the campers looked up at the trees around them. Could one of them be the creature?

"Trembling, my great-grandparents asked who she was and what she wanted. In a deep and hollow voice, she told them that her name was Gaea Everfree, an ancient spirit who held domain over the forest, and that my great-grandparents were trespassing on her land. They begged her to let them stay and build their camp, to share this wonderful place with others. Gaea Everfree finally agreed, telling them that she would leave the forest and allow them to build their camp, which they offered to name in her honor. But before she left, she warned them that they would not be able to keep it forever. Someday she would return and use all of the forces of nature to reclaim the forest as her own."

Timber told the campers of how Gaea hovered above the ground, summoning the winds, making waves swell on the lake, and sending bolts of lightning across the sky. As she disappeared, she left behind a glittering trail of jewel-like dust.

Fluttershy gulped. Spike nuzzled closer to her. Even Rainbow Dash's heart was beating faster.

"She kept her word," said Timber. *"Until now!"*

Rarity gasped.

"Strange things keep happening all over camp. And who knows? It could be the wind howling—or it could be the scream of a spirit. But if you see a trail of gem dust, you'll know that it is the return of Gaea Everfree."

No one moved. Everyone was spooked. A nearby bush began to rustle. Fluttershy screamed!

Gloriosa emerged from between some scraggly bushes, dusting leaves out of her hair. "Hey, guys! Sorry! Didn't mean to scare you."

Sunset Shimmer frowned. "Then why'd you come out of the bushes?"

"I took the scenic route because the forest is beautiful at night. But no one else should do it without a guide. Okay?" Her smile disappeared and she looked unexpectedly stern. "All right, everybody, time to head to your tents."

Snips bumbled over to where Gloriosa stood. "Do you have extra toothbrushes? I forgot mine."

"Sure do," chirped Gloriosa. "I'll get one for you."

Snails hung close to Snips. "I'm scared of the dark. Do you have flashlights?"

"Of course! I've got this." Gloriosa was ready for everything.

Fluttershy was staring into the fire, frozen with fear.

"Fluttershy, Fluttershy!" Spike barked. "Let's go."

"Sorry, Spike," she said. "I guess that story got to me."

Applejack shrugged. "Why? It can't be real."

But Rainbow Dash wasn't so sure. "I dunno; Gaea Everfree could be some creature that got booted from Equestria and ended up in this world. That's what happened with the Sirens."

The Sirens were a devious trio who came from the world of pony magic to Canterlot High to make trouble, until Sunset Shimmer saved the day.

But Applejack didn't think Gaea Everfree was anything to worry about. "Sounded more like something Timber was makin' up just to scare us." An owl hooted again. "Least I hope it was. Last thing I want is to have camp ruined by some power-crazed magical creature."

"Here, here," agreed Rarity. "We've had to deal with more than our fair share of those. At the Fall Formal, our musical showcase, the Friendship Games…"

Twilight felt uncomfortable. She'd made all the problems at the Friendship Games by experimenting with magic and turning into Midnight Sparkle.

Rarity noticed she was embarrassed. "I mean, everything turned out all right, of course," she backtracked.

"I'm kind of tired," announced Twilight. "I'm gonna turn in."

Spike hopped off Fluttershy's lap and headed over toward the Sapphire tent with Twilight.

When they were gone, Sunset Shimmer scolded Rarity. "Maybe lay off bringing up what happened at the Friendship

Games? I think she's still pretty sensitive about it."

Pinkie Pie poked her finger into a toasted marshmallow and spread the sticky sweet goo across her mouth. "Our lips are sealed," she mumbled.

Then she stuck out her tongue and licked off all the marshmallow. Delish!

CHAPTER

8

The Mysterious Case of the Crash Landing

★ ✦ ★

Twilight Sparkle was tossing and turning. She was having another nightmare. She murmured unhappily in her sleep.

She was dreaming that she was by the campfire again, toasting marshmallows. But she was all alone.

"Here I am," sang a high-pitched voice.

She whirled around, breathing hard, but no one was there.

"Over here," the voice teased from the opposite direction.

Twilight peered into the darkness, but she couldn't see anything. The fire crackled. Midnight Sparkle burst out of the flames. "I'm always here!"

"No!" screamed Twilight, jolting up in her bed in alarm.

"What is it?" Sunset Shimmer asked blearily.

Twilight looked around. It was almost dawn. She was in the tent—far away from the campfire. It had all been a nightmare. "Nothing. Sorry, Sunset."

But a more alert Sunset Shimmer wasn't reassured. "Uh, Twilight. I think something happened."

She pointed at Twilight's cot. It was float-ing in the air!

"*AAAAAHHHHHH!*" Twilight screamed again. The bed dropped with a thud.

Spike opened his eyes. "Is it time to get up already?" He snuggled back into the folds of the sleeping bag. "I think I'm just gonna snooze a little longer."

Sunset Shimmer was concerned. What was going on? "Twilight, we really have to talk about this—"

"No. We don't," Twilight interrupted her. She stormed out of the tent and headed down to the lake.

A few early risers were already out canoe-ing and boating as the sun rose.

Sunset Shimmer came up behind Twi-light. "Hey," she said gently. "I know you don't want to, but I really think we need to figure out what's going on with your magic. If you could learn to control it…"

Twilight whirled around. "But that's just it," she cried. "I'll never be able to control it."

Crash! An out-of-control boat sailed into the docks at full speed. The boat swamped, and the sailors were hurled overboard. Luckily, they had on their life jackets. No one seemed to be hurt. But the freshly built dock was destroyed. The lanterns were floating in the water toward shore. Pieces of wood drifted in the waves. It was a mess.

Timber rushed out of the boathouse to help the campers.

"What happened?" Rainbow Dash raced out of her tent.

Twilight was upset. "I didn't mean to…"

Sunset Shimmer stared at her, realizing something. "We didn't see it. So we don't know what happened."

She ran over to the kids staggering out of the water. "Are you okay?"

Fluttershy and Rarity appeared with towels.

Sandalwood dried himself off as he tried to explain what had happened. "It was so weird. We were stuck in the middle of the lake with no wind, then all of a sudden—*bam!* The wind picked up, and we were pushed right into the dock!"

Pinkie Pie gasped, her eyes wide. "You don't think it was the spirit, do you?"

"Spirit!" announced Trixie. "Show yourself. The Great and Powerful Trixie commands it!"

Nothing happened. Or rather nothing *seemed* to happen.

Rarity squinted, peering out toward the middle of the lake. "What's that?" She pointed.

A glowing trail seemed to divide the water in half.

"Is that crystal dust?"

"It's Gaea Everfree!"

"No way!"

"How else do you explain it?"

Everybody was talking at once—scared, excited, confused. What was going on? Had Gaea Everfree really returned?

"No," whispered Twilight to herself. "It was me." She slipped away from the other campers. She was upset.

Rainbow Dash went down to the dock to take stock of the damage. "Man! All our hard work. Ruined."

"At least the fishies are eating well."

Fluttershy pointed to a tub of fish food that had broken up and was floating on the lake.

"Let's salvage what we can out of the water," Sunset Shimmer suggested. "Maybe we can still fix this."

"We have to try," agreed Rarity. "Camp Everfree needs a runway."

"Dock," Applejack corrected.

Rarity sighed. "Yes, that's what I meant."

Sunset Shimmer noticed that Twilight Sparkle had disappeared. She had to get to the bottom of what was going on. It was all connected. But how?

CHAPTER

9

All Alone in the Woods

★ ✦ ★

Twilight wandered deep into the woods. She stepped over moss-covered logs. She wandered down a trail. She came to a secluded clearing near a small pond. She needed to think everything through by herself.

She'd been so lonely at Crystal Prep and so happy to transfer to Canterlot High. But was she destined to always lose control and make a mess of things? What was happening to her?

"It used to be so simple, the world I understood.

I didn't know what I didn't know, and life was so good.

Then I had to ask questions. The peculiar caught my eye.

And what I've seen can't be unseen. There is no way to hide.

Every time I think or feel, the monster inside proves to be real.

Even though I reach for the light, I can't escape Midnight.

Wrestling with the darkness takes its toll.

It's seen my face; it knows my soul.

How can I protect my friends, make sure my world doesn't end?

Even though I reach for the light, I can't escape Midnight."

She had come here to feel better, but instead she felt defeated.

Somehow the magic had gotten away from her and made that sailboat crash into the dock. What would happen next?

If only she knew.

CHAPTER

10

A Natural Nature Guide

★ ★ ★

Sunset Shimmer hurried back to the Sapphire tent. No one was around—except for Spike, who was still asleep. Sunset jostled his shoulder, trying to wake him up.

He murmured in his sleep. "So many squirrels."

"Spike!" shouted Sunset Shimmer.

He startled. He yawned. He looked around. "Ah, man, I was having the best dream," he said. "Wait! I'm in the middle of the woods. That dream could be a reality." He rubbed his paws together, imagining a day of chasing squirrels.

"Before you run off, do you have any idea where Twilight could be? I really need to talk to her."

"What happened?" Spike was suddenly concerned. "Did she do that lifting-things-off-the-ground thing again?"

"That's just it," said Sunset Shimmer. "I don't know if it was her. But if it was, we need to deal with it head-on."

Spike's nose wiggled. He sniffed. "I can track her down."

Meanwhile, far off in the forest, Twilight was trying to summon her courage to return to camp. But she couldn't calm down. She paced back and forth near the pond. "Keep it together," she told herself. "Deep breaths. You are not a monster."

"Nope," announced Timber, appearing beside her. "It's just Timber."

Twilight tried to pull herself together. "Oh, hi," she said as casually as she could. "What are you doing here?"

"Looking for you." Timber grinned at her.

"O-oh," Twilight stammered. "I just... went on a... nature walk. I got a little lost."

"Let me show you the way," said Timber. "I'm kind of an expert at these woods. I've lived here my whole life."

They began walking along a trail, side by side.

"That must have been nice, growing up at camp," Twilight said, trying to make conversation.

"Yeah, although it has its downsides. When I was younger, I wished we'd sell this place so we could live in town like normal people."

"Really?" Twilight was amazed.

"I was ten," explained Timber. "I really wanted to hang out at the mall." He smiled shyly. "I've never told that to anyone. You must be special, and not just because you have a tree branch in your hair." Timber gently reached over and pulled a small twig from Twilight's purple locks.

Twilight blushed. "How long has that been there?"

"Not long," answered Timber. "Just the whole time we were talking."

Twilight playfully hit him on the shoulder. "Why didn't you say something?"

He shrugged, laughing, and Twilight joined in. It was so easy for her to be with him.

They were so wrapped up in each other that they didn't hear footsteps coming toward them. They didn't even notice Sunset Shimmer and Spike, his nose glued to the ground.

"I guess we could help Twilight deal with the magic stuff a little later," Sunset Shimmer whispered to Spike.

"Don't want to interfere with the magic that's going on right now, am I right?" He held up his paw, and Sunset Shimmer slapped it in agreement.

"What did I say?" barked Spike happily.

Maybe Twilight Sparkle wasn't in as much trouble as Sunset Shimmer thought.

CHAPTER

11

Magical Mayhem!

★ ★ ★

Back at camp, everyone was challenging himself or herself to the climbing wall. One camper would stand at the bottom holding a safety rope called a belay while the other camper edged slowly upward, hand by hand and foot by foot. Everyone was wearing helmets and safety gear.

Applejack was holding on to her rope tightly and keeping a close eye on her partner, Rarity, as she climbed. Rainbow Dash was waiting impatiently for her turn. She was great at climbing!

Principal Celestia was explaining to everyone that climbing was such an important activity—not just physically but in terms of team building. "It's all about trust and perseverance. Rarity, you can trust that Applejack will spot you."

"Yeah, so you can totally go faster than you're going," Rainbow Dash called up to her impatiently.

"Rainbow Dash!" scolded Applejack.

"Sorry," Rainbow Dash apologized. "I've been waiting to do this since we got here!"

"Well," called down Rarity, hanging on

to a grip by her fingertips, "you'll have to wait a little longer, darling!"

Twilight and Timber Spruce emerged from the woods, side by side.

Rainbow Dash rushed over to her. "Oh good! Twilight, if you spot me, I can finally go! Be right back. I'll go get another climbing harness."

"Um, I'm not sure." Twilight hesitated.

But Rainbow Dash zipped off. Super fast. *Magically* fast. But no one noticed. Least of all Twilight. She only had eyes for Timber Spruce.

"I'd better make sure my sister doesn't need anything," he said to her. "See you later?"

Twilight nodded happily.

"Twilight," said Sunset Shimmer. "There you are. I was looking for you."

But before Twilight could answer, the ground beneath their feet trembled. It rumbled and roared and shook.

"Was that an earthquake?" worried Spike.

"We aren't near any fault lines," said Twilight.

Rarity was high up on the wall, clinging to it for dear life. The higher she got, the more scared she was. Even though the belay rope kept her perfectly safe, she didn't feel safe. Especially with that weird rumbling thing that had just happened.

"Hey," said Bulk Biceps. "Who left this crystal dusty stuff here?"

Rarity looked down at him from her perch. Bulk Biceps was bending over, examining a small glittering pile. She felt dizzy and more scared than ever. "I believe I'd like to come down now," she said.

Applejack pulled on the belay rope. But it was stuck. She pulled again. "Sorry." She yanked on it just a little bit harder—and Rarity was hoisted in her harness to the very tip-top of the wall.

Rarity screamed. Applejack screamed. Her hands came off the rope, and Rarity began falling. At the last possible second, Applejack grabbed hold of the belay, secured it, and Rarity didn't crash to the ground. Disaster averted.

Rarity was scared and furious. "Applejack, what are you doing?"

Principal Celestia rushed over. "Is everything okay over here?"

"I don't know what happened," said Applejack, confused. "I didn't even pull the rope that hard. It was like she was light as a feather all of a sudden."

Rarity unhooked herself from the belay rope. It was good to have her feet on the ground again, but she was still mad. "I was scared half to death!"

"It wasn't my fault!" insisted Applejack.

"I could have been seriously injured," said Rarity.

"Now, there's no need to exaggerate. You're fine. Let me help you get your harness off."

Rarity pulled away from Applejack, holding up her hands defensively. "No thank you!"

Applejack was about to help her anyway when a shimmering shield wrapped itself around Rarity. It was like crystal armor. Applejack pushed against it and fell backward into the lake. She spluttered, her mouth full of water. The strange shield disappeared.

"What in the world is going on?" Principal Celestia wanted to know.

Rarity had no idea. She looked down at her hands, shocked. "I'm so sorry. I think. Did I just do . . . whatever that was?"

"I don't think it was your fault." Twilight had been watching everything. She excused herself to go get Applejack a towel. Sunset and Spike hurried after her.

But Sunset Shimmer didn't think Twilight was responsible for this particular event. "You're not the only one with a new kind of magic! This is great."

Twilight stared at her. "No, it's not. Rarity and Applejack could have really hurt each other. Why is this happening? I don't…" Her voice trailed off as Gloriosa approached them.

"Hi, girls," she said, ever cheerful. "Anything I can do for you?"

"Applejack just fell into the lake," Twilight explained.

"Oh no!" cried Gloriosa. "She's gonna need warm towels, dry clothes, and a hot cocoa."

"She's more of a cider girl," Sunset Shimmer corrected. Something about Gloriosa rubbed her the wrong way. What was it? Could someone really be *too* helpful and *too* nice?

"I've got this," said Gloriosa, heading off.

A second later, there was an enormous explosion from the mess hall. *Bang! Bang! Bang!* Someone screamed. It was Fluttershy.

"Fluttershy!" gasped Twilight.

The girls raced over to the mess hall. It was a mess. A real mess. There was cookie batter on the floor, sprinkles on the tables, frosting on the walls, and Fluttershy and Pinkie were covered in cookie bits.

"What happened?" wondered Sunset Shimmer.

Fluttershy was baffled. "I don't know. We were just decorating cookies—"

"And I was all," interrupted Pinkie Pie, "'*You* need more sprinkles and *you* need more sprinkles.'"

Sunset Shimmer nodded. "Standard Pinkie Pie stuff."

"I was just tossing sprinkles to Fluttershy when all of a sudden they glowed pink and exploded!" Pinkie Pie grabbed another can of sprinkles to demonstrate. The moment it was in her hand, it began to glow hot pink.

Boom! It exploded. Cookie bits covered the ceiling—and Twilight Sparkle and Sunset Shimmer.

"Just like that!" Pinkie Pie giggled.

"Okay," said Sunset Shimmer, trying to think. "Why don't we lay off touching stuff for a while?"

Fluttershy wanted to get the mess cleaned up. She went over to the janitor's closet, where there were paper towels. But they were on a shelf too high for her to reach. "Can someone help me out?" she asked.

Before anyone could respond, a bird flew into the hall, fetched the paper towels in his beak, and dropped the roll right into Fluttershy's hand.

"Thank you, Mr. Bird," said Fluttershy in surprise.

The bird chirped.

"Why, of course I can get you a little some-thing to eat," she answered. She paused. Her mouth dropped open. "Did you just talk?"

The bird chirped again.

"But I don't speak chirp," said Fluttershy. "Or at least I've never been able to before."

Chirp. Chirp. Chirp.

The other girls watched in amazement.

"I don't know if you're the only bird I can understand," wondered Fluttershy.

Chirp.

"Oh no," Fluttershy begged. "Please don't call your friends."

But it was too late. A whole flock of birds flew into the hall, chirping and chattering.

"It's nice to meet all of you, too!" exclaimed Fluttershy.

Sunset Shimmer was stunned. "Were you just talking to the birds?"

"Yes?" Fluttershy wasn't really sure what was going on.

A door slammed. The birds flew out the window. Fluttershy screamed. But it was just Applejack and Rarity.

"Did you tell 'em what happened?" Applejack asked Sunset Shimmer.

"Haven't had the chance," answered Sunset.

Applejack sat down on a bench. "So crazy. I hoisted Rarity up the rock-climbing wall like it was nothin'. Like I had way more strength than I normally do."

Rarity nodded. "And I made a diamond-y thing appear out of nowhere. Which I'd normally be excited about. I mean, the facets were just perfect, and the clarity—"

"Rarity!" shouted Applejack.

"Sorry," Rarity apologized. "It knocked Applejack over and then it disappeared."

"Speaking of disappearing, has anybody seen Rainbow Dash? She went to get a harness and never came back." Applejack looked around the mess hall, noticing for the first time the hot-pink mess that seemed to be everywhere.

Boom! The mess hall door flew open. Fluttershy screamed. Again. Her nerves were just destroyed.

A blur raced past the girls and slammed smack into the wall.

"Owww!" Suddenly, Rainbow Dash collapsed on the floor.

"Whoa!" said Applejack. "How did you do that?"

Rainbow Dash rubbed her head, stunned.

"I don't know. I started running to get the harness, and the next thing I knew, I was practically back in town!"

"But if you have some kind of super speed, why were you gone for so long?" asked Rarity.

"Because I lost it when I got far away," Rainbow Dash explained. "And then it came back when I got close to camp."

Pinkie Pie's mouth opened wide. Her eyes sparkled. "Being at camp is giving us all new magical abilities!" she realized.

"I would have been perfectly happy with a souvenir T-shirt." Fluttershy sighed.

But Sunset Shimmer was thinking. "Not all of us have gotten new abilities. I haven't. But Twilight..." She paused.

Twilight was shaking her head, pleading with her not to say anything.

"But Twilight hasn't, either," she finished.

"So much for my theory that leavin' Canterlot High would mean leavin' any new magic business behind." Applejack did not look happy.

"Something at the camp must be making this happen," concluded Sunset Shimmer.

Fluttershy giggled nervously. "Gaea Everfree?"

The door creaked. It opened. A giant shadow loomed. Fluttershy screamed.

It was Gloriosa. She was holding a pile of fluffy towels.

"Applejack," she said, smiling. "I was looking for you! Here, I brought you some towels and dry clothes." Her face fell. "Oh dear. I forgot the cider."

As she was handing Applejack the towels and clothes, she noticed the mess.

It was hard not to. "What happened in here?"

Sunset Shimmer plastered a smile on her face and played dumb. "We're kind of trying to figure that out."

"Well, don't you worry about it," said Gloriosa. "I'll clean it all up in just a bit. I got this!"

Some campers ran into the mess hall. They were upset. "Gloriosa," said Sandalwood. "I kicked my beanbag into the lake."

"I'll get you another one!" she promised.

Another held up a sling filled with broken arrows. Gloriosa held up her hand. "Say no more. New arrows, coming right up!"

"There you are!" It was Timber Spruce. He'd been looking for his sister. "Filthy Rich is back. You want me to handle it?"

Suddenly, Gloriosa was all business. Her eyes narrowed. "Absolutely not." In an instant her smile was back on her face again. "I've got this!"

As she hurried out, she brushed past Sunset Shimmer.

"Fluttershy, enough with the screaming," Sunset snapped.

"I didn't scream," said Fluttershy, sounding confused.

"For once," Rainbow Dash added under her breath.

Rarity looked puzzled. "Nobody did."

The loudspeaker was crackling. Principal Celestia was announcing the next activity. "Attention, campers. Anyone who's interested in making floating paper lanterns, please meet us by the picnic tables!"

Applejack looked relieved. "I don't know about the rest of y'all, but I've been looking forward to comin' here for a month. Maybe we forget about this new magic for a bit and just try to focus on enjoying our time at camp."

"I was oh-so-excited about the designs I've come up with for the camp fashion show," added Rarity.

Rainbow Dash nodded in agreement. "And I've barely gotten to whup anybody in tetherball."

Sunset Shimmer was struggling. She loved nothing more than a magical problem— but she knew that her friends needed a break, too. "I think we should try to figure it out, but if letting it go for now is what the rest of you want…"

It was. They dashed around picking up

the worst of the cookie mess and headed out to go work on paper lanterns. Twilight hung back, a worried expression on her face. She couldn't let go of the certainty that this was, somehow, all her fault.

CHAPTER

12

Hiking After Sundown

★ ★ ★

The girls were busy making paper lanterns and decorating them. Pinkie Pie's was covered in marshmallows.

Rarity laughed. "Um, Pinkie Pie, what are you doing?"

"Putting marshmallows in my lantern!" she answered with enthusiasm. "Then when we light them, mine'll be beautiful *and* delicious!"

Rainbow Dash stared at her friend for a moment in concern. "You do realize that there's more to camp than just eating lots of marshmallows, right?"

Twilight was off by herself, working at a different table. Spike padded over to her, concerned. He cocked his head. He whimpered a little. "Hey, why aren't you with everyone else?" he asked.

A tear spilled out of Twilight's eye. "Sunset said something at camp is causing the other girls to get new magic." She lowered her voice to a whisper. "I think it's Midnight Sparkle. She's still a part of me, I can feel it. And I think her magic is infecting my friends."

"What are we gonna do?" Spike wondered.

"I don't know what I can do." Twilight felt overwhelmed.

Gloriosa was walking from table to table—getting glue, offering compliments, lending a hand. "Okay, everyone," she said at last. "It's time to watch your lanterns fly."

The campers headed down to the lake. Twilight's friends called out to her to join them. Twilight walked reluctantly over to the girls. But she tried to keep far enough away so no magic would happen.

Timber Spruce appeared. "Hey, cool lantern," he complimented her. "Mine's my face." He held it up. On one side he'd painted a silly face. Twilight smiled, but she was still distracted and upset.

"You okay?" asked Timber Spruce. "You don't seem like yourself tonight."

Twilight shrugged, but she didn't offer any explanation.

Gloriosa was ready for the big lantern send-off. "Ready?" she called. "And go!"

All the campers let go of their lanterns and they floated up into the sky. All except for Pinkie Pie's. Hers didn't go anywhere. It was too heavy.

Pinkie Pie grinned. "Oh well, now I get to eat it!" She took a big bite. "Yep. Beautiful and delicious."

Everyone laughed. That was Pinkie Pie's great gift. She lifted everyone's spirits. But not Twilight Sparkle's. She was just too miserable.

✷ ✶ ✷

Much later that night, after all the campers were in bed, Sunset Shimmer woke up and discovered that Twilight Sparkle wasn't in her cot.

"Twilight?" she called.

There was no answer.

Sunset Shimmer peered out of the tent window. The moon was rising. Sunset Shimmer saw a shadowy figure running toward the woods.

"Twilight?" she called again.

But there was no answer.

Sunset Shimmer headed out into the night. She raced after the figure. It turned off the forest path. She followed it. It disappeared through the trees. She followed it. It jumped out right in front of her!

Sunset Shimmer screamed. The dark figure screamed.

It was Twilight.

"What are you doing out here?" Sunset Shimmer wanted to know.

Twilight had Spike in her arms. "We're meeting a cab to take us home."

Sunset Shimmer couldn't believe it. She looked at Spike. Why hadn't he told her?

Spike shrugged. "She thought you'd talk her out of it."

"Because I would," said Sunset Shimmer. "Twilight, you can't leave." She reached out to take her friend's hand. But the moment she touched it, something strange happened. Her eyes flashed with sudden knowledge.

She remembered the trail of gem dust by the broken docks. She remembered Twilight disappearing. She saw in her mind's eye Twilight at the picnic table, worried about turning into Midnight Sparkle. That was it, wasn't it? Twilight was terrified of turning into a monster again.

"Twilight," she said sternly. "There is no Midnight Sparkle. There's only *you*."

"How did you know that was what I was thinking?" Twilight asked.

Sunset Shimmer thought for a moment. "When I touched your hand, I could see things. I could understand why you were leaving." Then it hit her. She got it. "My new magic! This is my new magic! This is incredible!"

"No!" shouted Twilight, even more upset. "It's not. I'm infecting you now!"

"Twilight, you have to stop looking at this as a bad thing."

"Easy for you to say!" Twilight's face crumpled. "Magic turned you into something beautiful. The last time I tried to use it, it turned me into a monster. I'm just so afraid it's going to happen again."

"Yeah, last time I turned into something amazing," agreed Sunset Shimmer, remembering how she had brought Twilight Sparkle back to reality at the end of the Friendship Games. "But I've let magic turn me into a monster, too. You heard what I did at the Fall Formal, right?"

Spike spoke up. "You tried to turn everyone into your own personal zombie army."

"Pretty much," confirmed Sunset Shimmer. "So, if anyone understands what you are going through, Twilight Sparkle, it's me. I can help you. And the rest of our friends can be there for you, too. But not if you run away."

Twilight considered what her friend had

said. At last, she answered. "I'll stay. But I still don't think it's a good idea for me to be near the rest of our friends right now. Not until we know why this is happening."

"Understood," Sunset agreed.

The girls began heading back to camp. The woods were quiet. All they could hear was their feet crunching over branches and leaves—until, *thud.*

"What was that?" Sunset tried to see into the darkness.

Very quietly, the girls tiptoed in the direction of the sound. A shaft of moonlight cast the shadow of a figure on the ground. The light glinted off steel. It was an ax. The figure was carrying an ax!

CHAPTER

13

Sparks in the Dark

★ ✦ ★

"Ahhhhh!" screamed both girls simultaneously.

"Ahhhhh!" screamed the ax-wielding shadow in response.

It was Timber. "Wait," he said. "Twilight?"

"Timber?" She sighed with relief. "I'm

so glad it's just you. What are you doing out here?"

"With an ax," added Sunset Shimmer.

"I was chopping down firewood," he explained.

The girls realized that right behind him was a large wagon filled with logs. But something wasn't right.

Sunset Shimmer was skeptical. "In the middle of the night?"

"We needed more for tomorrow night's campfire. And if I didn't take care of it tonight, it would just be one more thing Gloriosa would add to her list." He did a perfect imitation of his overeager sister. *"I got this!"*

Now it was Timber's turn for questions. "What about you two? Why are you hanging out in the woods in the middle of the night?"

Twilight was embarrassed. She didn't know what to say.

Sunset Shimmer stepped in for her. "I was sleepwalking," she lied. "Twilight found me and was bringing me back to camp."

"*Mmhmm.*" Twilight nodded.

Timber smiled warmly at Twilight. "You're a good friend. Come on. I'll walk you guys back. I'll protect you from...Gaea Everfree." He made all kinds of creepy sounds and said her name again. "Gaea Everfree."

"Come on," Sunset urged. "That's obviously just a spooky story you made up to tell around the campfire."

"Oh no," answered Timber Spruce. "It's legit. How else would you explain what happened at the docks? And that weird thing where the earth shook?"

Twilight glanced at Sunset. Could there

really be another source of the magic at Camp Everfree?

"Come on," said Timber. "I know a short-cut back to the tents."

He slipped his hand into Twilight's, and the two of them walked a little bit ahead together. Sunset noticed tiny sparkles of glitter trailing out of Timber's pocket. She lifted her finger and pointed it out to Spike.

"Legit, huh?" she whispered to the pooch. "I think we just found our Gaea Everfree."

Spike wasn't so sure. "But why would he work so hard to make us think she was real?"

"You heard what he said about wishing his sister would sell the camp. If nobody wants to come here because it's home to some angry ancient nature spirit, it sure would help his cause."

"We should tell Twilight," said Spike.

But Sunset stopped him. "Not yet. She's obviously going through a lot right now. We should probably be a hundred percent sure before we tell her the guy she likes is a jerk who's trying to run everybody out of camp."

Spike nodded in agreement. *Oh boy*, he thought, *it's time Twilight Sparkle had a break.* The last thing she needed was more trouble.

CHAPTER 14

A Superpowered Afternoon!

★ ✶ ★

Most of the campers were huddled around the picnic tables. Whenever the wind blew or a bird sang, someone would jump. Every now and then, one of the braver kids would look toward the shadows in the woods.

Gloriosa just couldn't figure out what was going on. "Why aren't you out there windsurfing?" she asked in concern. "Or making dream catchers? Or playing tetherball?"

Lyra and Trixie exchanged a knowing glance.

"We're not doing anything with some angry nature monster running around," Lyra told Gloriosa.

"The Great and Powerful Trixie," explained Trixie, "is totally creeped out."

"Nature monster? There's no nature monster," Gloriosa said sternly. Recovering, she added in an extra-sweet voice, "Please, everyone should be having fun. It was just a silly story. Now who wants to go windsurfing?"

One of the kids squinted, looking out at the water. "It's not even windy."

"Don't worry," chirped Gloriosa. "Just get changed and meet me there. I promise it will be super fun."

The campers shrugged. If Gloriosa was going to be there, maybe everything would be all right. They might as well give it a shot.

Down at the dock, Rainbow Dash and the other girls were back at work with repairs. Rainbow Dash had just carried a heavy plank. "Phew," she said, placing it down. She had walked very slowly across camp, as slowly as she could because she didn't want to take off again at super speed—but that made the work even harder. She looked over at Rarity, who was sewing something. "You gonna give us a hand here, Rarity?"

"Would really love to," answered Rarity. "But I really need to get the stitching on this poncho done if it's going to make it into the camp fashion show. Though at the pace you all are working, I don't know that the runway will ever be finished."

"The *dock*," Applejack corrected her. "The dock is our gift to the camp. And it's gonna get finished. That is, if Rainbow Dash would hurry up and bring me more wood."

Applejack was trying to nail a section of the railing onto the dock. She struck it gently, very gently, with her hammer—and nothing happened. She struck it again—very gently. Ten swings later, she managed to drive in the first nail.

Rainbow Dash was hesitant. "I can't go any faster," she complained. "I don't want to end up in the woods again—"

"Don't be silly," Applejack interrupted. Rainbow Dash pointed at Applejack's extra-careful hammering. She clearly didn't want to risk overdoing it like she had at the climbing wall.

"Really?" asked Rainbow Dash.

"I know I said we should try to forget about all this new magic business, but I can't." Applejack sighed. "All I wanna do is finish this dock, but I'm scared of using any of my strength. What if I hammer the board into splinters?"

"And I really want to help out," added Fluttershy. "But I'm afraid of what might come to help me." She had her eyes on a nearby squirrel.

Applejack was out of nails.

"Oh, here you go," said Pinkie Pie, tossing her a small pack.

"No!" screamed all the girls together, remembering the mess-hall mess.

Applejack dove away from the pack of nails like it was a grenade. She covered her head with her arms. Rarity produced her glittering diamond force-field cocoon. The pack of nails landed right next to Applejack.

"What?" Pinkie Pie wondered. Then she smiled, getting it. "*Oooh*, did you think the nails would explode like the sprinkles? Wow! Glad that didn't happen, huh?"

Rarity apologized for her force field. "Sorry, girls. I didn't mean to. I don't know how to control this."

"It's okay," said Rainbow Dash.

"None of us does." Fluttershy sighed.

"Which is why we shouldn't pretend this isn't happening." Sunset Shimmer had made a decision.

"Are you magic now, too?" asked Rainbow Dash.

"It started last night," Sunset Shimmer

revealed. "I can touch people and it's like I can feel what they're feeling and see their memories."

"Oooh!" squealed Pinkie Pie. "Fancy. Try me! Try me!"

Pinkie Pie grabbed on to Sunset Shimmer's arm. Sunset Shimmer saw pink cotton-candy clouds. It was like a movie playing in her head. She heard peppy party music. She saw a whole line of identical Pinkie Pies all diving at the same time into a giant swimming pool filled with fudge. They swam and kicked and danced. At last, there was only one Pinkie Pie. As she stepped out of the pool, a giant jelly bean handed her a towel. A marshmallow towel! Pinkie Pie gobbled it up.

Sunset pulled her hand free, laughing.

"So that's why you're always so happy," she said to Pinkie Pie.

"Yup!" Pinkie Pie grinned.

But Sunset Shimmer's glimpse into Pinkie Pie's mind made her realize something important. She turned to the group. "Girls, we can't just brush aside these powers because it doesn't seem like the ideal time to get them. What if it turns out that they could actually make things better?"

Rainbow Dash looked skeptical. Fluttershy seemed frightened. Pinkie Pie was the only one who seemed to agree with her.

"So you have magic," Sunset Shimmer sang to her friends. *"And it's not that great. But when it found you, it was fate. It's scary but it's wonderful, too. Just keep at it, and you'll agree. Embrace the magic, then you'll see. It's better once you know it's part of you."*

She smiled at Pinkie Pie. *"Oh, to have your energy! How amazing life would be! You can turn the everyday into a blast."*

Sunset Shimmer's eyes fell on Rainbow Dash. *"Super speed, it's so much fun. In five seconds, you'll get it done! You really know what it means to be fast!"*

Sunset Shimmer's words inspired Pinkie Pie, and she charged a small amount of sprinkles and placed them on the end of a wooden board. They exploded—making holes in the wood so they could be easily nailed together. In no time at all, Rainbow Dash was able to assemble them into benches. Pinkie Pie high-fived Rainbow Dash.

Sunset Shimmer was delighted. *"If you embrace the magic, there is so much you can do. If you just embrace the magic, you'll find a better you."*

Applejack took a breath. It was time to try out her superpowers. She picked up all the benches like they were twigs. There was a boulder in her path and she pushed it out of her way with her foot like it was a marble. She grinned from ear to ear. That wasn't so bad.

"Super strength, what's there to say?" Sunset Shimmer beamed. *"There's nothing standing in your way. Moving things with ease? It must be swell!"*

In her exuberance, Applejack didn't see a rope, and she tripped over it. Just as she was about to fall in the water, Rarity stretched out her hand and created a shimmery shield. Applejack landed on it and slid to dry land.

Sunset Shimmer clapped her hands. *"Crystal shield, it's more than bling. Protect your* friends from anything. Even if that something is themselves!"

Fluttershy was inspired. She carried the sign she'd been making over to the woods, and a flock of birds flew behind her. A bear appeared and helped her post the sign. The birds decorated it with flowers and vines. This was better than anything Fluttershy had ever imagined.

"Animals, they're mysteries," sang Sunset Shimmer. "To talk to them is quite a feat. I'm sure they have interesting things to say."

A bird trilled in Fluttershy's ear. Fluttershy nodded and laughed.

All of Sunset Shimmer's friends were magic. Magically magic.

"As for me," realized Sunset Shimmer, "I've got the touch. Close to someone, I can learn so much. It's a power I hope never goes away."

The girls were happy. They were ready to embrace the magic! They were ready to discover these strange new powers. They were ready to be themselves in a whole new way.

They worked on the dock. They sang together.

"If you just embrace the magic, there is so much you can do!"

Magic didn't have to be scary. It could be wonderful!

CHAPTER

15

Flash Forward

$$\bigstar \ \bigstar \ \bigstar$$

"Okay." Rainbow Dash grinned. "That was pretty awesome."

"And look what you managed to accomplish," Sunset Shimmer pointed out. The dock was finished! It looked just like the designs.

Rarity was thrilled. "Please, please, please, can we do a run-through for the fashion show on it right this minute?"

"Thought you weren't finished with the stitchin' on your poncho." Applejack sighed.

Rarity made a quick stitch. "I am now!"

Sunset Shimmer was happy for her friends, but there was one more thing she had to attend to. "Get started without me. I gotta go find Twilight. Seeing what we've been able to do here might make her embrace this new magic, too." She gulped, realizing she'd made a mistake. "Uh, not that she has any."

Sunset Shimmer headed back toward camp, past the boathouse, but stopped. The door was shut, but she could hear someone yelling. Someone was very angry.

"I just wish you hadn't told them that ridiculous story." It was Gloriosa.

Curious, Sunset Shimmer pressed her ear against the door to listen better.

"This is all too much for you," said Timber Spruce. "You have to let it go."

What were they talking about? Oh, she realized, he wanted his sister to sell the camp! He wanted her to get rid of it.

The door swung open and Sunset Shimmer barely missed being hit by it. Gloriosa stormed out. Timber Spruce followed his sister. When they were gone, Sunset Shimmer stepped out from among the shadows.

"Sunset Shimmer?" Flash Sentry had spotted her. "What were you doing behind that door?"

"What? Um...n-nothing," she stammered.

"I, um, lost an earring. Um, there it is!" She bent down and pretended to find something.

Flash fell for it. Something else was on his mind. "Hey, listen. I'm glad I ran into you. I really wanted to thank you."

"For what?" Sunset Shimmer wasn't listening very carefully. She was thinking about what she'd heard.

"For the tough love," said Flash Sentry. "Telling me I should get over Twilight. I needed to hear it."

"Sure," Sunset Shimmer said distractedly. "No problem."

"Is something wrong?" Flash noticed.

"What? No, why?"

Flash smiled at her. "Come on, Sunset, we used to date; I know when something's bothering you."

Sunset decided to confide in him. "Okay,

here's the deal..." she said. "My friend really likes someone, but I think that someone isn't who she thinks he is. I don't want to upset my friend by telling her what I think, but I also want to protect her, because if what I think is happening is really happening... then she deserves to know. You know?" She took a deep breath.

Flash was thoroughly lost. "No." Now Flash was distracted—by how the sun picked up the gold highlights in Sunset Shimmer's hair. "What I do know," he said, "is that your friend is lucky to have some-one like you to look out for her."

"Really?" Sunset Shimmer was surprised by his compliment.

"Yeah," he said. "You know, you've changed a *lot* since we went out. You're so much... nicer."

Sunset Shimmer was surprised. When they had dated, she had been different. All she'd wanted was power. She didn't know anything about friendship and how much magic there was in it. But it meant a lot to her that Flash had noticed. "Thanks."

Flash looked down at his feet, a little embarrassed. "You know, maybe you and me, we could start over...as friends..."

But before Sunset Shimmer could answer, she spotted Timber Spruce sneaking into the forest. What was he up to? She had to find out. She had to protect Twilight. "Sounds great," she said distractedly. "I gotta go." She took off in the opposite direction.

Poor Flash Sentry watched her disappear. "Cool." He sighed in disappointment. "I wanted to start over later, too."

CHAPTER

16

On the Mystery Trail

★ ★ ★

Sunset Shimmer was tracking Timber Spruce through the woods. She moved quietly; she was careful not to step on any twigs or dry leaves. She stuck to the shadows. She kept a safe distance back.

But she lost him. Somehow he managed to disappear.

"Shoot," muttered Sunset Shimmer. Where had he gone? She tiptoed through a stand of trees and looked over a cliff into a ravine. A dark figure was slipping into the open mouth of a cave. Who was it? It was definitely a human being and not a magical creature. But was it Timber Spruce? She wasn't sure.

A bolt of sparkling light shot out of the cave.

Uh-oh. Maybe somebody else out there was magic, too. Sunset Shimmer pulled out her phone and quickly sent a text to Twilight Sparkle.

Twilight was curled up on her cot with Spike beside her. She was reading a book when her phone buzzed. "It's Sunset," she told Spike. "She says to meet her by the rock quarry."

Spike looked worried. "I thought we weren't supposed to hike out that far."

"She says it's important," insisted Twilight.

Together, Spike and Twilight headed into the woods. They were just about to turn toward the quarry when pulsing orbs of rainbow-colored light appeared above them.

"What is that?" Twilight wondered, looking up at them. She didn't see the giant spiderweb right in front of her! She stumbled into it. She started to scream—but a hand covered her mouth.

It was Sunset Shimmer.

Waiting by the ridge, Sunset Shimmer had seen the strange lights. She held up her finger to her mouth to warn Spike and Twilight to keep quiet.

Twilight noticed the light coming from the cave.

"What's going on down there?" she whispered.

"I think it's Gaea Everfree—or rather, someone who wants us to think she's back. Come on," she urged.

Carefully, they made their way down the side of the cliff toward the cave.

"Who is it?" growled Spike.

Sunset glared at him.

"Oh," he apologized, slapping his paw over his mouth.

They were at the dark open mouth of the cave. Sunset held up her hand to stop them. She turned to Twilight. "Before we go in, there's something we need to talk about."

Twilight was confused. "Okay."

Sunset Shimmer took a deep breath. "You know how sometimes you think you know someone but really it turns out you don't because they have this deep, dark secret they've been keeping from you?"

Twilight's face fell. "Are you sure you're not talking about me?"

"No, definitely not you," said Sunset Shimmer. "But..." She just didn't know how to say it. She hated to break Twilight Sparkle's heart. She didn't want to tell her what she suspected about Timber Spruce.

They ducked inside the cave. They were totally unprepared for what they saw. It wasn't dank and gloomy; it was breathtaking. It was like being inside a kaleidoscope—glimmering crystals of all different colors decorated the walls. In the center of the cave were seven pillars—each festooned with sparkling gems and glittering geodes. It was awe-inspiring!

"This place is beautiful," whispered Twilight Sparkle.

"There's Equestrian magic here," Sunset Shimmer noticed. "I can feel it."

"Wait," barked Spike. "I thought Timber was just faking that there was a magical nature creature. Are you saying it's real?"

"Timber?" asked Twilight. "What does he have to do with any of this?"

Sunset was about to reply when someone else answered for her.

"Nothing." It was Gloriosa Daisy! "It's all me!"

CHAPTER

17

Out-of-Control Geodes

✦ ✦ ✦

Sunset Shimmer was confused. What was Gloriosa doing in the cave? Also, something seemed to be the matter with her. She was different, not herself...not cheerful at all.

"Gloriosa? But...Timber. I was sure he was the one making it seem like Gaea

Everfree was back. It was you who was trying to scare everyone away?"

Gloriosa looked shocked. "I would never try to scare anyone away from Camp Everfree!" she protested. "Never!"

Gloriosa pushed past Sunset Shimmer to get to the crystal pillars. Her touch triggered Sunset Shimmer's telepathy. Sunset Shimmer could see Gloriosa's thoughts—and what she saw completely surprised her.

Gloriosa was in a business office—and Filthy Rich was sitting on her desk. He was scolding her. "You fell behind on your payments, Gloriosa. I own the land now."

Gloriosa was almost in tears. "Please," she begged. "My great-grandparents founded this place. It's been in our family for generations. You have to let the camp stay."

"Instead of turning it into a spa resort that will line my pockets with more money than this camp ever could?" scoffed Filthy Rich as he stood up. "I don't think so."

"Please," Gloriosa pleaded. "I just need a little more time."

Filthy Rich's eyes narrowed. He chuckled. "Fine. I'll give you till the end of the month."

Gloriosa collapsed on her desk in tears.

Sunset Shimmer's eyes were shut. It made it easier for her to see the scenes from Gloriosa's life unfolding in her mind.

Gloriosa was running through the woods. She was crying. She didn't know what to do. A glowing bolt of magic from far away, from the direction of Canterlot High, arched over the forest—and landed right on the cave. Gloriosa stepped into the cave. She saw the seven glowing pillars. She touched one of the geodes, and magic light burst forth from it, bouncing off the walls, this way and that way, and hitting Gloriosa. She staggered backward. She was about to fall—but vines grew up from the ground of the cave and caught her. The pillars pulsed with light. Gloriosa reached out and pulled one of the geodes off a pillar.

Now Sunset Shimmer saw Gloriosa in the camp office arguing with Timber Spruce. She'd shown him the geode.

"You don't even know what those things are!" her brother had said.

Gloriosa had broken the geode into pieces and made a necklace of it. It glowed.

"But I know what they can do," Gloriosa fought back. "I've been practicing. I can control their power now."

Timber shook his head. "You don't know that for sure."

"This is our camp," Gloriosa yelled. "And it's being taken away. If this has to be our last week here, I'm going to use whatever it takes to make it count."

Gloriosa grabbed the camp microphone. Her voice echoed through the camp—and inside Sunset Shimmer's head. "Hey, everyone. If you could start heading to the courtyard, that would be rad. It's time to start the best week of camp ever!"

And Gloriosa was using her new magic to make sure that it was.

When she saw a few campers stranded in their sailboat in the middle of the lake, she touched her necklace and pushed her hands forward. A gust of wind blew up and sent the sailboat crashing toward the dock.

When a group of campers tripped over a rock on the trail, she touched her necklace and made the earth rumble. The rock shook free and rolled into the woods. The campers thought there had been an earthquake.

Timber Spruce was furious at her for playing around with magic. That's what their fight in the boathouse had been about. He had invented the story of Gaea Everfree to cover for his sister. He didn't want the campers to suspect anything. But Gloriosa thought it was a ridiculous story.

Sunset Shimmer's eyes blinked open. She understood everything now. "Timber wasn't talking about you letting go of the camp. He was talking about you letting go of the magical geodes," she realized. "All those things you were doing to make this week *the best week ever*, every time you used magic to do them, it caused another problem somewhere else. Timber was... covering for you!"

Gloriosa was stunned. How had Sunset Shimmer figured out all this? "How do you know about the magic?"

"I can see things," explained Sunset Shimmer gently. "Feel things. Because I have magic, too."

She pointed at Twilight. "And so does she. And so do our friends."

Spike shrugged. "I got nothin'."

Gloriosa startled. "Your dog can talk?"

"Okay," admitted Spike. "There's that. We usually try to keep it under wraps. Tends to freak people out."

Twilight approached Gloriosa. "Gloriosa, Timber wasn't wrong. Maybe you should stop using magic. Too much of it can be dangerous if you can't control it." The last thing she wanted was the camp director to suddenly turn into some crazed creature— just like she had.

"Oh, I got this," Gloriosa said confidently. "And I'm going to use it to save my camp. I just need more power!" She reached out her hand to grab more gems from the pillars.

"No!" Both Twilight and Sunset tried to stop her.

But Gloriosa used her magic to conjure a mess of creeping vines to tie up the girls. Gloriosa grabbed two more gems and added them to her necklace. Now there were seven crystals hanging there—one from each of the pillars.

The air was shimmering. Vines were creeping up Gloriosa's dress. Flowers were blooming in her hair. Where her eyes had been were swirling green orbs. "Sorry, girls," she sang in a mesmerizing voice. "I know what I need to do. But I feel like we're not on the same page, so..."

Sunset and Twilight struggled to free themselves from the vines. "No!"

But Gloriosa ignored them. She stepped out of the cave. She waved her hands. A boulder slid in front of the entrance. Twilight Sparkle and Sunset Shimmer were trapped.

CHAPTER

18

A Fashion Show Fiasco

★ ★ ★

Back at camp, the rest of the girls were getting ready for the fashion show. They were parading back and forth down the dock in Rarity's fashions. Rarity was the one who first noticed that Twilight Sparkle and Sunset Shimmer were missing. She had two outfits picked out especially for them.

"They're missing our dress rehearsal," Rarity fretted. She called for them. "Whenever you're ready." But there was no response.

But none of the other girls seemed concerned. They decided to start without them. DJ Pon-3 was spinning a record. Rarity made some final adjustments to the outfits. Applejack was admiring the stylish belt she was wearing.

"Told you you'd like it." Rarity laughed, pleased with her work and Applejack's reaction.

"It's all right, I guess," Applejack commented, trying to play it cool. "I do get to keep it after camp, though, right?"

Rarity grinned and sent Applejack strutting down the runway. Who'd have thought she'd be a natural model? But she was.

The girls were all too busy to notice the

strange creature floating toward the camp courtyard. Ivy trailed from her dress. Weeds tangled in her hair. It was Gloriosa. She was floating above the ground. She drifted past Snips and Snails.

"She looks different," noted Snips.

"You think so?" Snails asked, scratching his head.

More and more campers were heading down to the dock to watch the fashion show rehearsal. Timber was there, too.

"This is only a preview," Rarity told them. "I've got another entire line I'll debut at the real thing."

The record scratched to silence. "Why did you stop the . . ." Rarity's voice trailed off as she saw Gloriosa approaching. DJ Pon-3 was wide-eyed with amazement.

Campers started screaming.

"It's Gaea Everfree!"

"She's real!"

"We're doomed!"

Gloriosa grabbed the microphone from DJ Pon-3. "Attention, campers!"

Timber was in a state of shock. "Gloriosa? What are you doing?"

"That's Gloriosa?" Applejack couldn't believe it. "Am I goin' crazy or are her feet not touching the ground?"

Pinkie Pie tilted her head sideways to get a better look. "Freaky deaky!"

"I have an announcement to make," warbled Gloriosa, her voice strangely altered. "Filthy Rich wants this to be the last session of Camp Everfree... but don't worry. *I got this!*"

Gloriosa dropped the mic and pressed her hands to the ground. Red light spread out from her fingers, creating a huge circle around the entire campgrounds. Thorny brambles sprouted up, creating a defensive wall. They spread their branches, and their roots overturned tents and ripped down the just-built dock!

"Come on!" yelled Rainbow Dash. "We literally just finished building that."

Gloriosa was triumphant—and scary. "I've been searching for a way to keep the sharks in suits at bay! Magic has been my salvation, and now I can see that it's the only way to keep my camp with me!"

The campers were terrified and backing away from her. They tried to push through the wall of brambles, but it was too thick and prickly. They were trapped!

With a quick nod of agreement, Luna and Celestia charged toward Gloriosa. But she was ready for them. Vines sprang up, wrapped around them, and suspended them from a tree!

Gloriosa's green eyes sparkled. She was out of control! "I can feel nature agree. The camp should stay with me. But how to keep those tyrants out? A bramble fortress to surmount..."

Timber had found an ax and was chopping at the thorn bushes. For every branch he cut off, two more grew. The wall was bigger and stronger than before.

Gloriosa was ranting and raving. "We'll be safe in your thorny walls. And Camp Everfree will never ever fall. Nature, hear my plea; enshroud my camp for me!"

The brambles rose higher and higher— higher than the trees.

The campers were terrified!

What would she do next?

CHAPTER

19

A Thorny Problem

★ ★ ★

Gloriosa hovered in the air. Her arms were raised over her head. The brambles were taller, thicker, and darker. They cast huge shadows over the camp.

Fluttershy trembled. "Why do these kinds of things always happen to us?"

"I'm startin' to think it ain't Canterlot

High that's the magical element. It's us," said Applejack.

"What are we gonna do?" Rarity cried.

"What we always do," announced Rainbow Dash grimly. "Save the day."

The girls' eyes met. What else could they do?

Only one person was excited. Pinkie Pie. "Oh boy, oh boy, oh boy," she gushed. "This is gonna be so much fun! I only wish we had time to make superhero capes!"

"Me too." Rarity sighed. "I guess these incredibly chic ponchos will have to do."

"Enough about our wardrobes," Rainbow Dash snapped. "We've got to stop Gloriosa from trapping everybody in here."

The girls threw on their "capes" and leaped into action. Ears sprouted from their heads; their manes swished back and forth. The pony magic was on!

Rarity used her crystal shield to protect a group of campers from a twisting vine of brambles. Applejack summoned her mighty strength and hurled boulders through the wall. But it only grew back thicker than before. Rainbow Dash began running in ever-faster circles around Gloriosa, trying to confuse her. Pinkie Pie decorated the wall with exploding sprinkles. But no matter how many holes she opened, they grew back in a second. Gloriosa's magic was just too powerful.

Fluttershy called out to a crew of groundhogs. "Um, hi," she whispered to them. "Do you think you can give us a hand, er, paw? We could really use a way out."

The groundhogs nodded and began digging a tunnel under the brambles. Fluttershy quietly ushered kids over to it so they could escape to safety. Too late. The brambles filled the hole.

Gloriosa rose into the air. She rose above the whirl of dust Rainbow Dash had stirred up. She surveyed the campgrounds. She directed vines to stop Applejack. But Rarity protected her friend with her shield.

Next Gloriosa tried to stop Rainbow Dash. But Pinkie threw sprinkles on the attacking vines and Rainbow Dash scooted to safety.

But Applejack was worried. "None of this is working. Her magic is too strong!"

Campers huddled together, terrified.

The brambles were climbing higher and higher. They were arching toward one another. They were creating an enclosed dome of brambles. The campers were more trapped than ever. This was terrible. This was the worst thing that had ever happened to the Canterlot High kids. Gloriosa was the worst monster of all.

CHAPTER

20

Embrace the Magic!

★ ★ ★

Spike was gnawing through the vines that imprisoned Twilight and Sunset.

"Nice work, Spike," said Sunset, wriggling free. She studied the blocked entrance. "Twilight, you have to use your magic."

"I don't think I can lift something that big. Even if I can, I don't know for how long."

"It's our only chance of getting out of here and helping our friends," Sunset Shimmer pleaded.

Twilight closed her eyes and concentrated on the boulder. It wobbled. It shook. It lifted a tiny bit off the ground. Twilight concentrated even harder, with all her might. She got it up another foot. It was just high enough for the girls and Spike to slide under. It slammed down to the ground behind them when they were out.

Relieved, the girls hugged each other. The snap of a branch made them whirl around. It was almost as if they could hear the plants and the trees and the vines of the forest growing. What was that strange noise coming from near the lake?

★　★　★

Back at camp, each geode on Gloriosa's necklace was glowing. The brambles blocked the sun.

"Why are you fighting me?" she wailed. "I'm doing this to save our camp. I'm doing this for you."

The girls pretended to be listening. Meanwhile, Rainbow Dash was sneaking up behind Gloriosa.

"Gloriosa, let's think about all this for a moment, shall we?" Rarity was stalling for time. "I mean, I think Camp Everfree is absolutely delightful, but I just don't know that I'm ready to give up my weekly trips to the spa."

"To the spa?" screeched Gloriosa.

"Oh dear," Rarity whimpered. "What did I say?"

Rainbow Dash sped toward Gloriosa, but

she couldn't reach her. She was too high above them. She flew backward toward her friends.

Timber was trying to talk to his sister. "This isn't the way!"

"I appreciate your concern, Timber," Gloriosa bellowed. "But I got this!"

"No, you don't!" cried Timber.

The bramble bushes were still growing. They were creeping toward the campers. They were getting closer and closer. Soon there would be nowhere left to stand.

No one could get through to Gloriosa. She was transformed by desperation and by magic. Her eyes glowed vibrant and green.

Sunset and Twilight were stunned when they returned to camp—and couldn't get in. This was the sound they'd been hearing. It was the brambles getting bigger and bigger. Spike tried to gnaw a hole for them to get through, but it was no use.

"Twilight, do you think you can use your magic?" asked Sunset.

Twilight hesitated. "I don't want to use too much. Midnight Sparkle could take over."

"Our friends are in there," Sunset Shimmer reminded her.

Twilight focused her energy on the brambles. She concentrated. She shut her eyes. Slowly, a gap widened. It was just big enough for the girls and Spike to crawl through. But it closed right back up once they were through.

The first thing they saw was Timber begging his sister to stop. "Please, Gloriosa. What you're doing is crazy. You have to listen to me!"

"That isn't Gloriosa," Sunset Shimmer whispered to Twilight. She ought to know.

Magic had turned her into a monster before, too.

Relieved, the other girls noticed Sunset and Twilight. "You're okay!" gasped Rarity.

But Sunset was already talking to Timber. "That isn't your sister. It's someone who's been consumed by Equestrian magic."

Timber Spruce nodded. "Whoever you are, you have to let my sister go! Please, Gloriosa, come back! I need you!"

But Gloriosa stared at him haughtily as if she didn't know him.

The brambles were invading the campground. Kids huddled in tight clusters and tried fighting them back. They were even approaching Gloriosa. They'd wrapped their prickly vines around her legs.

"Gloriosa!" called Timber again, hoping to pull her back from the brink.

Applejack noticed the danger every-one was in and signaled to Rarity. Rarity enclosed everyone in a diamond dome. The brambles crawled over the surface of it. The thorns pierced the powerful substance and sent cracks rippling through it. It was only a matter of moments before it shattered.

Rarity was straining, trying to beat back the brambles. "I can't keep this up forever." She gasped.

"It's up to you!" Sunset Shimmer turned to Twilight in desperation. "You can use your magic to pull apart the brambles sur-rounding the camp."

"You have new magic, too?" Rainbow Dash was stunned.

"Why didn't you tell us?" asked Apple-jack.

Twilight was focused on the creeping

brambles. "No. There are too many of them. It would take too much magic. I can't."

"It's the only way!" urged Sunset Shimmer. "You have to embrace the magic inside you."

"But what if she takes over?" Twilight Sparkle worried. "What if instead of saving everyone, I turn into Midnight Sparkle and only make things worse?"

"That won't happen." Sunset Shimmer's voice was forceful. She meant it. "We won't let it."

Twilight Shimmer looked at the terrified campers. *Crack.* The diamond dome was breaking. She looked at Gloriosa, who was wild and out-of-control. She looked at the wall of brambles. She could do this. She had to. For her friends. This time it wasn't about power; it was about friendship.

Twilight closed her eyes and concentrated. The brambles edged backward, but they were clearly fighting the magic.

"Come on, Twilight!" said Sunset Shimmer. "You have to be stronger than she is."

Twilight's eyes opened. They were glowing—in exactly the same way they did when she turned into Midnight Sparkle. A unicorn horn emerged out of her forehead—just like Midnight Sparkle's. Black wings, just like Midnight Sparkle's, sprouted from her back.

Twilight wasn't Twilight anymore. She was Midnight Sparkle. She cackled devilishly. "You will never control me. I will always be a part of you!"

But when she blinked, the girls could tell that Twilight Sparkle was fighting back. "No!" she shouted.

"Twilight, listen to me," Sunset Shimmer commanded. "You are in charge!"

"You are a light, darling," Rarity told her. "A force for good."

"Yeah," added Rainbow Dash. "You can kick the darkness's butt!"

"We're here for you!" encouraged Pinkie Pie.

Fluttershy looked up at her friend, her eyes brimming with tears. "I believe in *you*!"

"You are not Midnight Sparkle," said Sunset Shimmer.

Her eyes blinked. One minute she was Midnight Sparkle. But then Twilight was back. "No," she struggled to say. "*I...AM... TWILIGHT SPARKLE!* And the magic I carry inside me is the Magic of Friendship!"

The Magic of Friendship is the most powerful magic of all. It was as if her words harnessed everyone's magic. All the brambles flew apart.

Gloriosa fell to the ground. "No! Stop!" Her necklace broke apart and magically divided into seven segments. Gloriosa's eyes fluttered and were no longer glowing green gems. She was herself again. Timber rushed over to her.

She barely knew where she was. "What happened?"

"It's okay," Timber Spruce told her. "It's gonna be okay."

The seven glowing rainbow-colored pieces of her necklace were floating up from the ground. They spread apart, each one headed to one of the girls. A swirl of light surrounded each of them. Instinctively, they reached for one another's hands. They were rising into the air. They were ponying up! Powerful white light beamed from their circle out toward the remaining brambles. The brambles vanished. They didn't grow back. They were gone.

The campers cheered.

The girls gently came back to earth. Their ears and pony tails were gone.

Spike leaped into Twilight's arms. "You did it!" He noticed her gem. "Hey! Nice bling."

"Awww," gushed Rarity, seeing them together.

Each of the girls reached up and touched her neck. They were each wearing one of the geodes as a necklace.

"What are these?" Applejack wondered.

"I'm not sure," said Sunset. "But clearly we have some kind of connection to them."

"I almost don't care what they are.

They're gorgeous," enthused Rarity. "And will totally go with the other collection I was working on for the camp fashion show." She noticed the broken dock, the exhausted campers. "That's probably canceled, isn't it?"

But maybe it wasn't after all.

CHAPTER

21

A Crystal Ball

★ ★ ★

There was a lot to clean up. But everybody was ready to help—especially Gloriosa. She was devastated with what she'd done. "I am so sorry," she apologized to everyone. "I only wanted this to be the best week Camp Everfree has ever had, and instead I've made it the worst." She hung her head.

"Maybe it's for the best that I'm losing the camp to Filthy Rich."

"No, it's not," said Principal Celestia. "This camp has meant so much to so many people. My sister and me included."

"Why do you think we wanted our students to come here?" Vice Principal Luna added.

"It's an absolute tragedy that future generations won't get to experience it," said Celestia.

Twilight heard what they were saying— but she couldn't accept it. "No!" she blurted out. "We can't let Filthy Rich take this place away!"

Everyone looked to Twilight.

She took a big breath. "If camp meant so much to you two, maybe it meant as much to the other campers who came here in years past."

Sunset Shimmer's eyes lit up. She got it. "And maybe we can get them to help save it!"

"Like a fund-raiser or a benefit?" asked Applejack.

"Or a ball!" Rarity exclaimed.

"Our band could play," suggested Rainbow Dash.

"I could write a song just for the occasion," said Fluttershy.

Pinkie Pie started jumping up and down. "I could make cupcakes with sprinkles! Just regular sprinkles, not the exploding kind."

Gloriosa couldn't believe it. "Those are all good ideas, but where would we hold it? The mess hall isn't big enough!"

Sunset Shimmer grinned. She had just the solution. "We could hold it in the Crystal Cave!"

"A Crystal Ball?" punned Rarity with a grin. "I love it!"

Still, Gloriosa wasn't sure. "I admire everyone's enthusiasm. Really, I do. But I just don't know how we're going to plan a ball by tomorrow and invite everyone."

The girls glanced at one another, smiling. "We got this!"

And they did. It was just going to take a little extra Friendship Magic.

"I used to think that stories were just that.
Set in stone, concrete as a fact.
It didn't come to that I could change history.
Now I know I write my own,
Fight my way to the ending that I want.
I'll turn a tragedy to an epic fantasy!

Hey, hey, hey.

You can be a hero, too.

Take my hand; I'm here for you!

Come, come away with me.

Be the legend you were meant to be!

You are and always will be Everfree!

There was a time when fear held me down.

I let it chain me to the ground.

But now I'm soaring. Life is never boring!

I'm as awesome as I wanna be.

But I'm more than I believed.

Faster than lightning and more exciting,

We'll be a sight you can't miss,

Just trust in us 'cause we got this!

We're always sure to win. If we harness the power that's within."

Back in the mess hall, Pinkie Pie was dancing from here to there getting campers to help her with the baking and snack-making. She couldn't resist charging up a few sprinkles with magic and having them explode like fireworks. They were so pretty, and they rained down on the cupcakes, decorating them perfectly. Everyone clapped. Pinkie Pie took a bow.

They each had their special talents, and they were learning how to use them. Sunset had empathy—she understood what people were thinking and feeling. Fluttershy could connect with the animals and talk to them. Rainbow Dash was like a superhero. She had speed! Rarity was a force of protection, and Applejack was mighty! Twilight could move anything with her mind, and Pinkie Pie was Pinkie Pie! She was explosive! Together they made a team.

Soon the stars were out and the moon had risen. Lots of people had heard about the Crystal Ball. They began arriving in their ball gowns and tuxedos. Everything looked so magical. Just outside the cave was a donation box (that looked a lot like one of the fish-food boxes from the dock).

A crystal chandelier hung from the ceiling of the cave, lighting up the crystal and the gems and the pillars. At the back of the cave was a stage. The Sonic Rainbooms were tuning up their instruments and getting ready to play.

Rarity thrummed her keytar. Fluttershy shook her tambourine. Applejack let loose with some power chords from her bass. They were ready to rock!

"Come, come away with me.

Be the legend you're meant to be!

You are and always will be Everfree*!"*

The audience clapped wildly. More people dropped donations into the box. Gloriosa took the stage. "Thank you all so much for coming. And for helping us raise enough money to save Camp Everfree!"

There were cheers and more clapping. No one noticed when a scowling Filthy Rich turned on his heels and slunk out of the cave.

Gloriosa looked with gratitude at the Sonic Rainbooms. "Thank you. For everything. If I'd just asked for help in the first place—"

"Don't sweat it," interrupted Rainbow Dash cheerfully. "It's kind of what we do."

Later on in the evening, DJ Pon-3 spun some discs and people danced the night away. Twilight used her magic to restring some twinkly lights that had fallen. Timber came up beside her.

"Not to brag or anything," he said, "but it's pretty cool how I saved all the campers from those *Rubus fruticosus*." He noticed Twilight's blank expression. "Blackberry brambles."

Twilight smiled. "I'm familiar with the genus. It's just a little weird you'd say you saved the campers. I thought I saved them."

"Yeah," said Timber playfully. "But I saved you from falling on the dock so that you could save the campers. So, technically, it was all me."

Twilight burst out laughing. "I'm really glad I met you."

"Uh-oh." Timber sighed.

"What?"

"That sounds like a good-bye, and here I was hoping we'd still be able to hang out. Maybe get dinner and catch a movie?"

Twilight's face lit up. "Yeah. I'd really like that."

"Oh good," said Timber. "I was hoping that's what this meant." He pointed to the string of lights—they were all floating in the air! Twilight blushed.

"This is awesome!" Timber reassured her.

"It kinda is, isn't it?" admitted Twilight.

Gloriosa interrupted them. "Oh, uh, sorry. I need to borrow Timber. There are some donors I really want him to meet. They were good friends with Mom and Dad," she explained to Twilight.

"Save me a dance, okay?" asked Timber.

Twilight nodded happily.

"Adorable!" gushed Rarity, who'd seen everything.

"He does seem like a pretty cool guy," Sunset Shimmer said.

"Know what else is cool?" Everyone looked at Rainbow Dash. "Our awesome new superpowers. I handed out, like, four hundred fliers, set up the stage, got all our instruments, and still had time to pick up a pizza. I *love* my super speed!"

Sunset Shimmer nodded. "About that. I think the crystals are the source of those superpowers."

Fluttershy reached up and touched her necklace protectively. "You're not gonna ask us to give them up, are you?"

"No. In fact, I think maybe we were meant to have them all along."

"Me too," agreed Twilight unexpectedly.

A flash of anxiety crossed Sunset Shimmer's face. "There is one thing I'm still wondering about, though..."

"What's that?" Twilight asked.

"Where did the magic that hit this cave come from?"

But nobody knew the answer.

Nobody knew that after the Friendship Games, the portal between the worlds wasn't really shut all the way. A tiny sliver was open between Equestria and Canterlot High—and through that tiny, almost invisible thread of a portal, colorful wisps of magic were pouring into the world of the Equestria Girls.

Every day Canterlot High was becoming more and more magical. What would happen next?!

Sunset Shimmer and the Canterlot High
gang are heading to Camp Everfree,
and so are you!

Turn the page for some fun camp activities!

Five Minutes to Midnight...

Twilight Sparkle is *soooooo* worried that she might turn into Midnight Sparkle again. Every time she sees her reflection in the mirror, she checks to make sure she's not sprouting wings or growing a unicorn horn. Can you lend a helping hand? Can you help spot which Twilight is about to turn into Midnight Sparkle?

PACK YOUR BAGS!

You are headed to Camp Everfree! Principal Celestia has told you to bring a flashlight, sweater, and sneakers, but what are *your* must-bring items? Are you taking along extra marshmallows like Pinkie Pie? Or do you have a spare ball gown tucked into your suitcase like Rarity?

1 _____

2 _____

3 _____

4 _____

5 _____

WHAT ARE *YOUR* SPECIAL MAGIC POWERS?

Each girl discovers her inner magic
at Camp Everfree. Sunset Shimmer is
sensitive, and she can hear people's
thoughts. Fluttershy has always been good
with animals, but now she can talk to them.
What is your special magic?
Describe the powers it gives you.

_____

_____

_____

_____

_____

_____

_____

Imagine your special magic getting you in trouble like Rainbow Dash and Applejack! What happens?

_____

_____

_____

_____

_____

_____

_____

_____

_____

_____

_____

DeCoRate tHe DOCK!

It's time to help out with the
camp gift! The new dock is built...
but it's not painted or decorated.
How will you make it look extra pretty?

CAMPER SCRAMBLE

Everyone's all mixed-up after
Gaia Everfree takes over the camp. Can
you find the missing Canterlot High kids?
Unscramble the names of the campers.

AHFLENSSYRT

....

BBCIPSUKLE

....

EKPIINEIP

....

PSNSI

....

SSLNIA

....

Answer Key: Flash Sentry, Bulk Biceps, Pinkie Pie, Snips, Snails

SPOOKY STORIES

Gather 'round the campfire! It's time to tell the tales that give everyone shivers and goose bumps. Rarity tells a story about a fashion disaster, and Timber Spruce scares the campers with the legend of Everfree. What is your story going to be about? Will it have ghosts and haunts? Will Gaia Everfree return? Brainstorm some ideas for your very own spooky story for your friends and write them here.

_____

_____

_____

_____

_____

_____

More S'mores!

Pinkie Pie wants to share her special recipe with you for the stickiest, yummiest, bestest campfire treats ever...Magical S'mores.

"You need lots of marshmallows. Lots. A whole bag. Maybe another bag. Did I say lots? Can you ever have too many marshmallows? No! (Remember: A bag of marshmallows can be a pillow, decorate a bird house, or just make you happy!)

"You need graham cracker cookies and thin milk-chocolate bars. Got it?"

- *Marshmallows*
- *Graham crackers*
- *Milk-chocolate bars*

1 Put your marshmallow on the end of a stick and roast it carefully with adult supervision! Make sure every side is golden brown and the insides are extra gooey!

2 Put a piece of chocolate on top of one of your graham crackers.

3 Add the hot marshmallow goo on top! (It's going to melt the chocolate! *Mmmmm!*)

4 Put another graham cracker on top to make a sandwich.

5 Gobble it up…and make more! That's why they call them…S'mores!

and SHe's off!

Rainbow Dash is racing to put up posters for the Crystal Ball all over town. Can you get her to town as fast as possible?

START | HeRe

FINISH

WRite Stuff

It's time to giggle! Rewrite this event
from the book with your own funny words.

Applejack was holding on to her rope _____ and keeping a
                                        (adverb)
close _____ on her partner, Rarity, as she climbed.
        (noun)

Rarity was high up on the wall, clinging to it for dear life. The

higher she got, the more _____ she was. Even though the
                            (adjective)
_____ kept her perfectly safe, she didn't feel safe. Especially
(noun)
with that _____ _____ that had just happened.
            (adjective)   *(noun)*

Rarity looked down from her perch. She felt _____
                                                (adjective)
and more _____ than ever. "I believe I'd like to come
            (adjective)
down now," she said.

Applejack _____ed on the belay rope. But it was stuck.
            (verb)
She _____ed again. "Sorry." She _____ed on it just
        (verb)   *(verb)*
a little bit harder—and Rarity was hoisted in her harness to the

very tip-top of the _____.
                        (noun)

Rarity screamed. Applejack _____ed. Her _____
                                (verb)   *(noun)*
came off the rope and Rarity began falling.

a Letter to Mom and Dad

Imagine you are on the Canterlot High school trip to Camp Everfree. A lot has been happening. A lot! Imagine you are writing a letter home to your parents to tell them about recent events. What would you tell them about Gaia Everfree?

ENJOY MORE MY LITTLE PONY FUN WITH EQUESTRIA GIRLS MOVIES, NOW ON BLU-RAY AND DVD!

THE ADVENTURES CONTINUE WITH LEGEND OF EVERFREE COMING NOVEMBER 1ST

outKids.com

HASBRO and its logo, MY LITTLE PONY EQUESTRIA GIRLS and all related characters and logos are trademarks of Hasbro and are used with permission. ©2016 Hasbro. All Rights Reserved.